THE BATTLE OF THE RED HOT PEPPER WEENIES

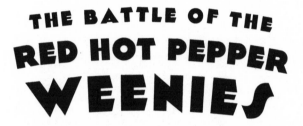

AND OTHER WARPED AND CREEPY TALES

STARSCAPE BOOKS BY DAVID LUBAR

Novels

Flip

Hidden Talents

True Talents

Story Collections

The Curse of the Campfire Weenies,
and Other Warped and Creepy Tales

In the Land of the Lawn Weenies,
and Other Warped and Creepy Tales

Invasion of the Road Weenies,
and Other Warped and Creepy Tales

THE BATTLE OF THE
RED HOT PEPPER
WEENIES

AND OTHER WARPED AND CREEPY TALES

DAVID LUBAR

STARSCAPE

A TOM DOHERTY ASSOCIATES BOOK
NEW YORK

THE BATTLE OF THE RED HOT PEPPER WEENIES AND OTHER WARPED AND CREEPY TALES

Copyright © 2009 by David Lubar

Reader's Guide Copyright © 2009 by Tor Books

"Bad Luck" originally appeared in *Sunscripts*, 2004.
"Time Out" originally appeared in *Boy's Life*, May 2004.
"Braces" originally appeared in *Orson Scott Card's Intergalactic Medicine Show*, September 2007.
"Just Like Me" originally appeared in *Orson Scott Card's Intergalactic Medicine Show*, March 2007.

A Starscape Book
Published by Tom Doherty Associates, LLC
175 Fifth Avenue
New York, NY 10010

www.tor-forge.com

ISBN-13: 978-0-7653-2099-5
ISBN-10: 0-7653-2099-1

First Edition: March 2009

Printed in the United States of America

0 9 8 7 6 5 4 3 2 1

For M. Jerry Weiss, Helen Weiss, and Don Gallo,
the true champions of the short story

CONTENTS

CONTENTS

CONTENTS

A BRIEF WORD OF INTRODUCTION

I need to thank several people, and apologize to a whole lot of others. Feel free to skip this part if you aren't one of them—though you'll never know for sure unless you keep reading. It's difficult to get one book of short stories published. The fact that I have four is a miracle. The miracle workers are my publisher, Kathleen Doherty; my editor, Susan Chang; and my publicist at Tor, Dot Lin. I'm a lucky guy. My wife, Joelle, and daughter, Alison, gave me lots of feedback for these stories, and never complained too much about being in the presence of a compulsive story writer. More luck on my part.

Bill Mayer, the artist who draws those amazing Weenies, deserves a lot of credit for the popularity of these collections. It would be impossible to name all the people who work to get the book from me to you, including distributors, booksellers, and the guys in the warehouse, but it would also be impossible not to thank one person in particular. Ed Masessa has done amazing things for the Weenies.

The teachers and librarians who share my stories with their students deserve my thanks, as do all of you young readers who've told your friends or your teachers about my books.

Speaking of young readers, I guess this is as good a place as any to apologize to all the seventh-grade boys who might not be amused by a certain line in one of the stories. (You'll know which line I mean when you read it.) I was just kidding. Honestly.

Onward. Enjoy the stories. Don't read them in the dark. You won't be able to see the words.

THE BATTLE OF THE
RED HOT PEPPER
WEENIES

AND OTHER WARPED AND CREEPY TALES

ALL THE RAGE

Kieffer Loomis was the only kid in our whole school who never got angry. He was so calm, it was spooky. I'm no hothead myself, but life dumps tons of bad stuff on everybody. Some of it isn't fair. Some of it is just plain rotten. For example, I yelled at my little sister Jilly last week when she colored all over my library book with her crayons. She started to cry, which made Mom angry, which got me in trouble, which made me even angrier.

I didn't stay angry forever. And Mom took the library fine out of Jilly's allowance. So it all worked out. But I'd never seen Kieffer even raise his voice.

There are a couple of ways to deal with any behavior that's too weird to ignore. You can figure it out, or you can change it. I started by trying to figure it out. Two weeks ago, I went over to Kieffer at lunch and asked, "How come you never get angry?"

He looked at me like that was a stupid question. "What do you mean?"

"You never lose your temper," I said. "How do you stay so calm?"

Kieffer shrugged. "I guess that's just the way I am. When something bothers me, I swallow it."

"Swallow it?"

"Yup. You should give it a try."

That didn't sound like it would work. But I had a chance to find out for myself the next day. When Bobby Thugger pushed me down on the playground, I sat there and tried to swallow my anger. I could feel it swelling in my throat. Nope. I knew right away that it wouldn't work. My anger was too large, and my throat was too small. I got up and pushed Bobby. That felt a lot better. So much for swallowing my anger.

As I said, there are two ways to deal with weird behavior. One way is to ask about it. The other is to change it. Or, in this case, do something that most boys are really good at—see how far you can push it. I don't know who came up with the idea, but this morning a bunch of us—me, Dwight, Alan, Richie, and Patrick—decided that our only goal in life was to make Kieffer lose his temper. We were going to break his calm, big-time.

"No matter what, don't give up," Dwight said as we waited in front of the school.

"Nope. Total attack," Alan said.

"But it can't look planned," I said. "It has to look like accidents."

"There he is." Patrick pointed across the lawn at Kieffer, who'd just reached the school yard.

"Me first." Alan charged toward Kieffer at full speed. When he got close, he shot his hands out and shouted,

"Tag! You're it!" He shoved Kieffer harder than I'd ever seen anyone get tagged outside of a professional wrestling ring. The poor guy flew at least five or six feet before he landed on his butt. After landing, he slid a couple more feet. By then, Alan had dashed away.

Kieffer looked around like he had no idea what had just hit him. His face grew expressionless for a moment. His jaw clenched, like he was going to shout. Then, even from a distance, I could tell he was swallowing. It looked like he was choking down a golf ball.

You're doomed, I thought. That had just been a warm-up. We had the whole day ahead of us. I ran to the wood shop and grabbed a screwdriver while the teacher wasn't watching, then headed for the lockers. I jammed the blade into the edge of Kieffer's locker and twisted, hoping I could mess up the door enough so it wouldn't open. Then I backed off and waited.

It turned out I did a pretty good job jamming things up. Kieffer tried to open the locker. It wouldn't budge. He raised his fist like he was going to punch the door. Then he sighed, swallowed, and walked off.

Life grew worse and worse for Kieffer throughout the morning. After lunch, we got other kids involved so he wouldn't suspect our group. By the end of the day, the whole class was taking turns making him miserable.

Still, amazingly, he swallowed every bit of his anger.

Maybe we just couldn't get mean enough. But on the way out of the building, Alan did the tag thing again. This time, he did it on the stairs, catching Kieffer from behind.

I winced as Kieffer went tumbling. As much as I wanted to see him explode, this was a bit too rough.

I guess the fall had stunned him. He lay there on his back, staring up at the clouds. Nobody moved. Finally, I stepped forward to give him a hand. I figured that would be a nice thing to do, even if the guys got mad at me.

Just as I was about to reach out and say something friendly, I noticed Kieffer's lip was twitching. His jaw moved like he was trying to swallow, but his head jerked like something dry and jagged was caught in his throat.

Maybe we hadn't lost, after all. The anger was finally too much for him to swallow. But he hunched his shoulders, clenched his fists, and gulped. I could swear I saw a pulsing lump slide down his throat—a big wad of swallowed anger, moving like a fat rat through a slim snake. I guess Kieffer's anger still wasn't too big to swallow.

But it was too big to stomach.

Kieffer's shirt rippled, like someone was punching at it from the inside. He stared down at his gut and moved his lips. Faintly, I heard him say, "Oh, no . . ."

The anger burst out—all of it—years of swallowed anger. It exploded from inside him. Kieffer's anger was dark and wet, with shiny scales that hurt to look at. It had claws like saw blades and teeth that dripped green venom. As it swelled, it let out a howl that made my eyes bleed and my teeth crack.

Some of the crowd froze, or dropped to the ground. Some turned to run. It didn't matter. Kieffer's anger was everywhere. As I spun away, I felt a burning slash rip across my back. My legs went numb. I fell. I dragged myself a foot or two with my hands and elbows, then gave up and flopped on my chest.

My vision was fading. I could see Kieffer, not far away. His eyes were glazing over. The screams all around me had turned into whimpers. Anger had destroyed all of us.

"Sorry," I whispered.

Kieffer smiled.

How could he possibly be happy? "What?" I asked. That was as much as I could manage to say.

"It felt good to let all that anger out," Kieffer said.

I'll bet it did. As I closed my eyes and sank into the darkness, I realized the weirdest thing. I wasn't angry at all.

FRANKENDANCE

What's wrong, Sunshine?" my dad asked me. My name is Lily, but he likes to call me names like Sunshine and Princess.

"Nobody asked me to the dance," I told him. "Every other girl in my class has a date. Even Sabrina Zimanski, who spits when she talks and drools when she breathes. It's the first school dance ever, and nobody wants to take me."

"Oh, stop worrying your pretty head," Dad said. "I'm sure you'll get a date."

"No, I won't. I'll never get a date."

"Yes, you will. I promise. When is this dance?"

"A week from Saturday."

"That soon? I'd better get back to the lab. I have a lot to do." Dad dashed for the attic steps. He had a lab up there where he invented things.

I cried myself to sleep that night as thunder shook the walls of my bedroom and rain fell like my own tears.

The night before the dance, Dad insisted on taking me to the mall to buy a new dress.

"But I'm not going to the dance," I said.

"I promise you, you'll go," Dad said.

I let him buy me the dress. I figured I could wear it some other day.

"Try on your dress," Dad told me on Saturday evening, half an hour before the dance.

"No. That would just make me sad," I said.

"It would make me happy," Dad said. "Please."

I went to my room and changed. When I got back, there was a big guy in a black sweater standing next to Dad. As I got closer, I saw that he had one blue eye and one brown eye. His ears were different sizes, and one of them was sort of rotated a bit so the earlobe pointed toward his nose. At least I think it was a nose. It was in the right place, and had two holes, but beyond that, the resemblance was kind of weak.

"This is Stitchy," Dad said. "He's taking you to the dance."

Stitchy smiled and waved at me. I noticed his little finger and ring finger were switched.

I sniffed the air. Something rotten made my nose twitch. It reminded me of the pack of month-old hamburger meat I found in the back of the fridge last year. "He smells."

"You're in seventh grade," Dad said. "All the boys smell. Right?"

I had to admit that Dad had a point. By the end of the evening, the whole gym would smell like the inside of an empty clam chowder can that had been sitting in the sun. "Do you know how to dance?" I asked Stitchy.

He nodded, grunted, then twitched like he'd been hit by lightning.

"Okay—let's go." Why not? He was still better-looking than most of the boys in my class, except for Brandon Kratchweiler. He's totally gorgeous. Not that he even knows I'm alive.

"Have a wonderful time," Dad said.

"We'll try."

We headed out. Stitchy actually held the door for me. *This might work*, I thought. Though I was pretty sure I wasn't going to dance with him.

The school was only three blocks from my house, but Stitchy didn't walk very quickly. I guess it would have been easier for him if his legs were the same length. The left one was longer, so he kept angling toward the road. I had to turn him back every time he reached the curb. By the time we got to the school, the gym was already crowded.

Nobody paid any attention to us. That was fine. I found an empty table and started to sit down, but Stitchy held up a hand to stop me. Then he pulled out a chair and pointed to the seat.

He waited until after I sat down to take his own seat. I watched the other kids. Everyone was dancing to a fast song. When the music stopped, Brandon Kratchweiler strolled over to my table, along with a couple of his friends.

Brandon pointed at Stitchy. "Where'd you dig him up?"

I didn't say anything. It was hard to talk, or even think of any words, when I was this close to Brandon.

Brandon smiled at me. "You make a nice couple. . . ."

I tried to get my lungs to help me say, "Thank you."

"A real nice couple," Brandon said. "A couple of total losers." His smile shifted to a smirk. Behind him, his friends laughed.

As a different pressure crushed my lungs, Brandon turned toward Stitchy and said, "Man, how can you even show your face? That's one weird-looking nose."

Stitchy moved faster than I'd ever seen him move before. He shot up from his seat and grabbed the top of Brandon's head in one hand. It looked like when those professional basketball players palm a ball. Stitchy lifted Brandon straight up. As Brandon kicked and screamed, Stitchy grabbed Brandon's nose with his other hand.

"No, Stitchy, don't do it!" I shouted. No, wait—that's a lie. To be honest, I pretty much whispered it.

Stitchy yanked real hard.

Whatever sound Brandon's nose made must have been pretty sickening. Luckily, Brandon's scream drowned it out.

Stitchy dropped Brandon, turned toward me, and held out his left hand. He pointed at the nose in his palm; then he pointed toward home and made a sewing motion.

"Sure, I suppose Dad could put it on for you," I said. "But I kind of like you the way you are."

Stitchy raised one eyebrow. I guess he raised it too hard, because it fell off.

I picked up the eyebrow and put it in my purse. "Really. You don't need to change. You're perfect without that snooty old nose."

Stitchy raised the other eyebrow. It stayed on. I nodded.

Stitchy tossed Brandon's nose over his shoulder. It landed in the punch bowl. Brandon, who had stopped screaming but was still moaning and whimpering a lot, raced after it. I gave Stitchy a napkin so he could wipe his hand.

The DJ put on a slow record. "Come on, Stitchy," I said, "let's dance."

Stitchy and I walked out to the dance floor. He held me close. So I held him close, and danced. We moved in slow circles—clockwise, of course.

As we danced, I couldn't help thinking how lucky I was. Some of the other girls at the dance might have nice guys, or guys who they thought were perfect for them. But out of all the girls in the gym, I was the only one who could honestly say that my guy was made for me.

THE RATTY OLD
BUMBER∫HOOT

The first rumble of thunder struck just as Woodrow was stealing the comic book. He froze, looked around, then slipped the comic from the middle of the pile. "That jerk will never miss it," Woodrow muttered. It served Dwayne right for bringing the comics to show-and-tell and bragging about how many he had. Woodrow's mother didn't approve of comics, so he didn't have any of his own. But these were too awesome to resist.

Woodrow stuck the comic in his desk and joined the rest of his class outside for recess. When they got back, he watched Dwayne carefully. Sure enough, the fool never checked through the stack.

Perfect, Woodrow thought. At the end of the day, he waited until everyone else had left, then slipped the comic under his shirt and headed out.

The rumbles grew closer. A raindrop hit Woodrow's nose. He looked up at the sky just as the clouds let loose. A heavy rain fell, and wind slapped at his face. He hunched over and ran for the nearest shelter—a porch on an old house to his left.

The rain seemed to grow even harder. Woodrow shivered and watched the water rushing into the gutter across the street. He jumped as the door behind him opened. He spun and found himself facing a plump old lady with frizzy white hair and red cheeks. She looked like someone who baked lots of cookies.

"Do you want to come in?" she asked.

"No." Nearly every day, in school and at home, Woodrow was warned about strangers. Besides, his favorite show was starting in ten minutes. "I have to go."

"Well," the woman said, "you aren't dressed for this kind of weather. You'll get soaked to the bone."

Woodrow glanced at the lawn, where the grass was already turning into a land of miniature lakes. The woman was right. The rain would soak right through his shirt. He didn't care if he got wet, but the comic would be ruined. He'd dropped a magazine in his bathtub once. The pages had gotten all warped and rippled, and they'd stayed that way even after they dried out.

"But I really need to get home," he said.

The woman looked over her shoulder, and then back at Woodrow. "You wait right here, young man."

She scurried off. There was a clatter and a bit of banging; then she returned with a smile and an umbrella. "You can borrow my ratty old bumbershoot," she said. "I'm not planning to go out in this downpour."

"Bumbershoot?" Woodrow asked.

The woman laughed. "Silly me. I guess it's an old-fashioned

word. But I'm an old-fashioned lady." She thrust out the umbrella. "Here. Take good care of it."

"I will." Woodrow pushed the umbrella open and held it over his head with one hand. The fabric smelled like old people. The handle was white, like ivory. The shaft was some sort of polished dark-brown material. He pressed his other hand against his chest, keeping the comic in place. The umbrella was large enough to cover him like a canopy. The tips of the ribs dropped past his shoulders.

Leaning against the wind, Woodrow stepped off the porch. The splat of water against the umbrella nearly drowned out the woman's next words. "You be sure to come back," she said.

"I will. I promise." Woodrow didn't want to keep her stupid umbrella. Which didn't mean he'd go to the trouble of bringing it back. He planned to chuck it in the trash once he got out of the rain.

The wind whipped up, jerking the umbrella in his hands. One of the end tips scratched his cheek. Woodrow swore and grabbed the handle with both hands, keeping his arm pressed against the comic so it wouldn't fall out from under his shirt.

The wind gusted again. The umbrella twisted and flapped like it was trying to fly back home. "You can borrow my bumbershoot," Woodrow said, mocking the woman's voice. "Yeah, sure, I'll bring it back. Stupid old lady . . ."

Another gust nearly tore the umbrella from his hands. He pulled it closer, tilting it so he could see well enough to know where he was going.

For a moment, the umbrella was strangely still. Then it

flapped and jerked again. As the snap of the fabric filled his ears, Woodrow realized something was missing.

No rain.

The sound of the raindrops had stopped. The puddles around him were unrippled. The umbrella jerked and flapped.

Woodrow didn't hear leaves rustling. He didn't feel his pants legs flapping. No wind. The storm was over.

In the instant that it took Woodrow to wonder how an umbrella could flap when the air was dead calm, he lost his chance to fling it away. By the time he tried, it was too late. The umbrella clamped down on him with a wet snap. As the stiff fabric encased him, Woodrow struggled to free his arms. A dozen sharp jabs ringed his body as something bit into his flesh.

Woodrow let out a muffled scream. He kicked. He fell to the ground and rolled. It didn't matter. Nothing could make the bumbershoot let go of him. Not until it was finished.

When the wind picked up again, blowing back toward the house, the ratty old bumbershoot let go of what little remained, and tumbled back home, leaving behind nothing but a damp pile of clothes, a soaked pair of muddy shoes, and a wet, ruined comic book. As it bumped back against the porch steps, a small moist sound came from among the flaps. It might have been a burp.

DEAR AUTHOR

"Class, we are going to write letters," Ms. Twilliger said.

Everyone groaned. Nobody writes letters anymore, except kids whose parents make them write letters to thank their aunts and uncles for stupid sweaters that don't fit and look so ugly even a dog wouldn't want to wear them.

But my attitude changed when she added, "You'll each write a letter to your favorite author."

Now that was sort of cool. I loved Digby Morgenstern. He wrote the best books. My favorite was *Snot Rocket*, about a kid who could go places by sneezing real hard.

I was afraid Ms. Twilliger wouldn't let me pick Digby Morgenstern, because she doesn't seem to think much about books that involve anything wet or drippy. But she said that was fine. Actually, what she said was, "If you absolutely can't think of anyone else."

We also had to follow these stupid rules. In the first paragraph, we had to introduce ourselves. I guess that made sense. In the second, we had to tell the author three things we liked about his book. In the third, we had to list three things we didn't like. I felt that this was a really stupid thing to ask us to do. Who wants to hear complaints? *Dear Author, your book stinks because nothing at all happens in the first chapter except that the main character gets dressed. And then, in chapter two, he looks in a mirror and describes himself.* Yeah, that would go over big.

But I wrote my letter. Here it is:

Dear Mr. Morgenstern,

I'm your biggest fan. My name is Tommy Zwinger, and I love your books. I even got in trouble once for reading one, because it made me laugh so hard that I farted during SSR. That's Sustained Silent Reading. We do that every day. A silent room is pretty much the worst place to fart. And this one was a real monster. I almost shot out of my chair. I guess you could call me Fart Rocket.

Here are three things I love about your books. First, they make me laugh. Second, they are funny. Third, lots of humorous things happen in them.

I hate to tell you, but there are also three things I don't like about your books. First, they are too short. (They are so good, I always want more.) Second, there aren't enough pages in them. Third, they could be longer.

Thank you for reading my letter. Please write back to me so I can get extra credit. I know you are busy, but I could really use all the help I can get with my grades.

Your biggest fan,
Tommy Zwinger

So that was my letter. Now let me tell you three things I don't like. First, Digby Morgenstern never wrote back to me. Second, Ms. Twilliger gave me a C– on the assignment. And third, a year and a half later, Digby Morgenstern came out with a book called *Fart Rocket*. It's about a kid named Tommy who gets in trouble for farting while reading a funny book during SSR.

I told everyone he'd stolen my idea. But I didn't have a copy of my letter, so nobody believed me. That didn't matter. I wasn't going to let him get away with it. So I wrote him another letter. This time, I didn't bother listing three things I liked about his books. I just came right to the point.

Dear Mr. Morgenstern,

You stole my idea. Remember me? The original Fart Rocket? I hate you. I told everyone it was my idea, and they all made fun of me. They called me Liar Boy. All day long, they hold up stuff—books, staplers, even rocks— and say, "Hey, is this your idea, too? Did you invent air? Did you invent water?"

I'm getting really sick of it. You could at least have given me credit in the book. It's too late for that now. But you could write back to me and admit it. If you don't, I'll be miserable for the rest of my life.

Your former fan,
Tommy Zwinger

He didn't write back to me. I survived. Kids still mock me, but not constantly. Especially not since Walter Sphinxter took up yodeling as a hobby and Charlene Ebbermeyer decided it would be fashionable to dress like a pilgrim. But then, a year and a half after I wrote the second letter, Digby Morgenstern came out with a book called *Liar Boy*. You can guess what it's about. Yup—a kid who writes to an author and gets his idea stolen, but nobody believes him. He didn't give me credit this time, either. But I'm keeping my mouth shut. And I'm sure not writing him another letter.

THE WIZARD'S MANDOLIN

Cicarelli was the greatest wizard in Florence. Citizens came to him from all over Europe for spells, potions, and advice. They believed his magic arose from the herbs he gathered or the words he muttered from behind his long beard. In truth, they didn't care all that much about the source, as long as the magic worked. And, in truth, they were wrong about the source.

Cicarelli cast his spells with his mandolin. All it took was the right combination of notes. An A-flat combined with a C-sharp might cause the potion he was brewing to bring its user wealth. A D-minor chord could turn the same potion into a cure for poison. A tremolo on an open E string might help transform a curse into a blessing. Cicarelli knew only one spell he could cast—or uncast—without his mandolin. But that was enough.

Daminieri was an unexceptional wizard, mediocre at best, who wanted Cicarelli's power. For years he lurked in shadows and listened to rumors. At last, through bribes, treachery, and skulking talents a rat would envy, he uncovered the secret of the mandolin and vowed that he would steal it and become the most powerful wizard in Italy.

A half hour before sunrise, when wizards are at their weakest but the unexceptional are not all that much changed, Daminieri crept into Cicarelli's home and lifted the mandolin from its peg on the wall. *It isn't guarded*, he thought, amazed at his good fortune. He crept back out to the street and then scurried to his shack at the edge of the city.

There he sat, with the mandolin in his hands. "I will discover all of your secrets," he whispered.

He placed one hand on the neck and the other by the sound hole. He pressed the strings against the fret board, forming a G-major chord, and strummed.

The music was not pleasant.

"It is flat," he muttered. "I would think Cicarelli would keep his instrument in tune."

"No," said a voice from outside his window. "It is sharp."

Daminieri clutched the mandolin tighter as he recognized the speaker. He turned toward the window and found himself face-to-face with Cicarelli.

"Very sharp," Cicarelli said. There was a note of sadness in his voice.

Daminieri looked down at his hands. His face grew pale as he saw what the sharp strings had done to his fingers. His face grew even more pale as blood poured from his wounds.

Cicarelli stepped in through the door and took the mandolin from Daminieri's hands—or what was left of them. "You'll live," he said. "Unless you try to steal from me again."

He uncast the sharpness from the strings and wiped the blood from the neck with a cloth. Then he carried his mandolin home where it belonged.

INTO THE WILD
BLUE YONDER

I thought I was out of luck when they canceled the local carnival this year. I love stuffing my face with carnival food like deep-fried candy bars and corn dogs, and then going on extreme rides that fling you upside down so fast that parts of you don't catch up until an hour later. There's nothing like a high-speed tumble with a gut full of grease to test whether you really have a strong stomach. So far, I've passed every challenge. Nothing makes me sick.

But last year, some forty-year-old guy who watched too many action movies tried to jump from one horse to another on the merry-go-round and broke his leg. He sued the town. He didn't win, but the town spent a ton of money on lawyers, and refused to allow another carnival.

I thought all was lost until Buzzy Skantz came stomping up my porch this morning. "Ryan! Hey, are you there?" he shouted. He banged on the door, yelling, "Bang! Bang! Bang!"—just in case I didn't realize someone was seeking my attention.

"What's up?" I asked when I got to the door.

"There's a carnival over in Lakewood," he said. "My mom's going to drop me off. Want to come? Don't be a bum, chum."

I would have instantly shouted, *Yes!* but Buzzy is kind of hard to hang out with. He reminds me of those comedians who shout everything instead of talking. Unlike the comedians, though, he isn't funny. Just loud.

On the other hand, a good carnival is so loud, I might not even be able to hear Buzzy. "Sure. I'll go."

"Baboom!" he shouted, thrusting his arm in the air like he'd just won an Olympic gold medal. "We're on. We'll pick you up at seven. Not eleven. It'll be heaven." He ran off the porch, making race car noises.

What have I done?

I told myself it would be fine. The memory of funnel cake, cotton candy, and supersweet lemonade eased my worries.

Buzzy swung by at seven that evening. I was waiting on the porch. I could have been waiting inside a locked safe buried in a pit in my backyard and I wouldn't have missed him.

"Ryan! We're here! Get it in gear! Or I'll kick your rear!"

Did I mention Buzzy thought he was a hip-hop star? I got in the car and thanked Mrs. Skantz for the ride.

She nodded and turned up the radio, real loud. Lakewood was a thirty-minute—or a one-hundred-twenty-shout—trip. But at the end of it, sure enough, there was a carnival, full of food, rides, and games.

"Have a good time," Mrs. Skantz said as she pulled up near the entrance. "I'll be back for you at ten. Remember to stay away from the food. You know it makes you hyper." She handed Buzzy five dollars.

That's not going to go far, I thought. Everything at a carnival is expensive.

"Sausage!" Buzzy screeched as he leaped from the car. He went running toward the first booth—Sonny's Super Sloppy Sausage Sandwiches. They must be good sandwiches—there was a mob of customers. Buzzy ducked under some elbows, dodged around a couple people, and disappeared from sight. He popped back into view seconds later with a sandwich in his hands. By the time I reached him, he'd already devoured half of it.

"Bite?" he asked, thrusting the chewed end toward my face. "Tastes just right. Pure delight."

"No thanks." I stood back for the twelve seconds it took him to gobble down the remaining half. I liked sausage, but I wanted something sweeter. As we walked away from the booth, I saw the sausage seller glaring at Buzzy.

"Rides!" Buzzy shouted. He sprinted toward the midway. I stopped at a booth and bought some ride tickets, then followed him to the Scrambler.

"You go ahead," he said.

That was weird. I gave the ninety-year-old guy who ran the Scrambler my ticket and climbed into one of the open cars. While the guy was checking that everyone was strapped in, Buzzy snuck past the gate and slipped onto the seat next to me.

So that's how he planned to stretch his five dollars. What a slimeball. I wondered whether he'd stolen the sausage, too.

It turned out the Scrambler was a big mistake. Spinning in the air with a shouter who still has bits of a Super Sloppy Sausage Sandwich in his mouth isn't a great thing to do if you're wearing a white T-shirt.

"Another ride?" Buzzy asked when we staggered off the Scrambler. "Let's stay outside. Don't try to hide."

"In a while. I want to get some food." And I didn't want to get in trouble if he tried to sneak onto another ride. I followed my nose to the funnel cake stand and bought myself a sugar-covered mass of deep-fried happiness.

Just as I was picking up my plate from the counter, Buzzy grabbed my shoulder and shouted, "Open wide! I found the coolest ride!"

The jolt sent my funnel cake sliding off the paper plate into the dirt. As I was wondering whether I could pick it up and brush it off, two little kids ran right over it.

"Let's go!" Buzzy shouted, tugging at me. "You're slow. Can't say no." He dragged me over to a really run-down-looking ride at the far end of the midway.

The sign in front, made of large individual flaking red letters that dangled from a crossbar above the entrance, read, WILD BLUE YONDER. The Y was hanging at an angle like it was ready to drop off. The rusted ride might have been blue a long time ago, but it sure didn't look very wild. It was basically a small jet with two seats on a shaft that could swing in different directions. The jet itself looked like it could rotate on the end of the shaft. Not bad—but I really didn't want to be next to Buzzy when I was being shaken all over the place.

Scratchy music played from somewhere at the base of the ride. I recognized the song. It was the air force theme about flying off into the wild blue yonder. Okay—so the name sort of made sense.

A dozen kids were lined up, waiting their turn. There was a gate right inside the entrance. Kids moved inside the gate after they gave the guy their ticket.

"You go ahead," I told Buzzy.

"Okay. Hey, look!" He pointed over my head. As I turned, he stuck his foot in front of me and shoved me from behind.

I let out a shout as I tripped and fell into the only mud puddle in the whole carnival. A couple people came over to help me up, including the guy who ran the ride. He looked a lot like the guy who ran the sausage booth. Maybe they were brothers. After I got to my feet, I saw Buzzy at the front of the line. He'd hopped the gate.

The guy glanced at Buzzy, but didn't say anything. He just let him on. Before the next kid could get in, the guy said, "One at a time."

The ride started out slowly, then picked up speed. In a moment, it was really swooping around. It looked cool enough that I almost wished I was on it. Then again, I could always ride it after Buzzy got off.

"It's not *mild*!" Buzzy shouted as he swooped past.

I noticed that the letters in the name shook. On his next swoop, Buzzy shouted, "You're such a *child*!"

The letters shook again. But not all of them. I realized it was just the *I, L,* and *D.* That was weird. They bounced like someone had given the support post a hard kick.

As Buzzy shot past again, he yelled, "This is *wild*!"

The letters in WILD shook, then fell off the crossbar, one at a time. The *W* barely missed the head of a kid who was standing in the line.

Buzzy was now riding the BLUE YONDER.

"Me!" he shouted as he swooped by. "I'm riding."

Next swoop, he pointed at me. "You're *not*!"

The *N* and the *O* in BLUE YONDER shook. There wasn't a *T.* I wondered whether letters would fall only if they matched the whole word. Not that it mattered—as long as nobody was standing underneath the sign, nobody would get hurt.

Buzzy ran through a half dozen rhymes for *not*, and then shouted, "You don't have a *clue*!"

As the *L*, *U*, and *E* shook, my eyes locked on the sign. I'd always been good with word games. What I saw made my knees buckle. I could feel the blood drain from my face. I realized that Buzzy's words might matter a lot. *Don't say it*, I thought. But I knew it was coming. He was running out of other words.

"The ride's not *through*!"

I wondered if there was any way I could get him to be quiet.

"You belong in a *zoo*!"

Just the O shook.

"Go buy a *canoe*!"

I glanced at the ride operator. Maybe the ride would end before Buzzy said the wrong thing. I hoped so. But the guy was standing there with his arms folded across his chest like he was willing to let BLUE YONDER run all day.

Buzzy pointed at me and screamed, "I'm better than *you*!"

Oh, no. He'd said it. *You*. I looked at the sign. The Y fell first, leaving BLUE ONDER. The U fell, leaving BL E ONDER. Finally, the O dropped. The sign now read BL E NDER. The crossbar was still shaking enough to make the letters slide together. Buzzy was no longer riding the BLUE YONDER. He was strapped into the BLENDER.

I hoped nothing else would change, but I sort of knew what was coming. The jet tilted so its nose pointed straight up. The wings folded down. The tail turned into a blade that pulled into the bottom of the jet.

I flinched as a whirring sound ripped through the air. I heard Buzzy scream, *"Help!"* His scream was followed by sounds I didn't want to identify.

The whir slowed, and then stopped. The ride, still shaped like a blender, lowered itself to the ground and settled into the base. I heard a liquidy sort of slurping, like when water runs down a half-clogged drain.

I noticed a thick hose attached to the base. I followed it with my eyes, though I really didn't have to. I was pretty sure I knew where it led. The hose, snaking its way among the dozens of cables and wires that cross a carnival ground, ran all the way to the rear of Sonny's Super Sloppy Sausage Sandwich booth. I guess Buzzy was headed there himself.

I wasn't in the mood for any more rides. And I really wasn't in the mood for any food. I headed to the parking lot to wait for Mrs. Skantz. It was going to be kind of hard to explain about Buzzy. I guess I was sorry we'd come to the carnival. But I was pretty glad I didn't eat the sausage.

YACKITY-YAK

Hey, I'm sorry to bother you, but I have to talk to someone. We're both waiting for the bus anyhow, so I hope you won't mind. I don't think the next one's coming for a half hour. Okay if we talk?

"Great. I'm Linda, by the way. I think we go to the same middle school. I've seen you in the halls. You might have seen me, but I'd understand if you didn't notice me. Nobody notices me. That's how my big problem started. I was getting all sad and depressed because it seemed I'd have to go through life just not being popular or anything. Then I found this book in the used-book store. It had fallen behind one of the shelves. I had the feeling it had been there for ages. It was a book of spells.

"I know that stuff can be dangerous, but I was sort of desperate. So I looked through it, and there was a whole section of social spells, like how to make a guy fall in love with you, and how to win a contest. But I really didn't want any guy to fall in love with me at the time, and there wasn't any contest I needed to win. I just wanted a better social life.

42

"I found a spell that promised to make me fascinating. I knew that would do the trick. Hey—I notice you keep looking at your watch. So I guess you already figured out that I'm not fascinating. I'm my usual old boring self.

"If you guessed that I messed up the spell, you're right. The ingredients were pretty simple, except for the bat's wing. I'm not even going to tell you how I got one of those. Anyhow, I mixed it all up in a copper bowl, just like the book says, then put it in a shallow pan in the oven. Luckily, it's not something you have to drink. No way I'm drinking anything that's got a bat's wing in it. You just boil it up, and then wait for it to cool and dip your left hand in it.

"So I did all of that, and I'm all set to be popular. But the moment I dipped my hand in the mixture, I started talking. I guess you've noticed I've barely stopped to take a breath.

"What's this about? I ask myself. I check the spell really carefully, and I notice that I was supposed to use a toadstool taken from a graveyard. But I guess what I used was a mushroom or something. I'm not even sure what the difference is. The point is, I didn't cast the spell I wanted. So now I don't know what to do.

"That's a nice watch, by the way. I guess we've been here for a while. The bus should be coming pretty soon.

"Anyhow. I looked through the book, page by page, and I found another spell that was close to mine. This one was just like the one for popularity, except that it used a mushroom instead of a toadstool. As I said, I really don't know the difference. But, obviously, I ended up making the wrong spell. Unfortunately, this one wasn't in the social section. It was in the section for dealing with enemies.

"This spell lets you talk. Actually, it makes you talk. So

here I am, forced to keep talking. I've been talking for three days, now. I can't stop. Let me tell you, this is definitely not the way to become popular. I'm sure not messing with any more spells. Not ever.

"But the good thing is that the spell doesn't last forever. It's pretty easy to remove. Well, maybe not pretty easy, but it can be removed.

"Oh, look, the bus is coming.

"Anyhow, all I have to do to remove it is find someone who will listen to me for half an hour. Well, actually, it doesn't get removed. It sort of gets transferred.

"I guess I don't have anything else to say. Thanks for listening. What's that? I'm sorry, I really don't feel like hearing anyone else's chatter. Gotta go. Bye."

WISH AWAY

Alien or genie—it was hard to tell. All Michael knew at first was that the creature wasn't human. It appeared at midnight in his room, with the sound of a handful of mud thrown against his window. It began as a shadow against the wall, cast through the curtains by the sliver of moon. The shadow grew thicker, gained grayness and hints of color, and took the form of a twisted man with the head of a venomous snake.

Michael screamed and scooted back until he was wedged deep into the corner of his room. But the creature caught the sound with his flickering tongue and swallowed it.

"Hush," he said. "There is nothing to fear."

"Who are you?"

"A wishmaster."

"What?" Michael realized his fists were still clenched. He let his fingers uncurl.

"Call me Somna," the creature said. His voice was deep, like the rumble of thunder, but quiet, like the whisper of cloth against cloth. "I'm here to admit you into the League of Wishers."

"What's that?" The only league Michael knew about was the one at the bowling alley.

"Special people with a special talent. There are those in the universe who can make their wishes become real." Somna pointed a claw at Michael. "It is a rare talent, and one that requires training. It is my task to find those who possess this skill and teach them to master it. Are you ready?"

Michael nodded, though his mind was numb.

"You've already begun," Somna said. "It was a wish that brought me here. You called me when you yelled about the unfairness of life. It was a powerful call."

Michael remembered the tantrum. His joystick broke right after dinner. He'd asked his parents to take him to the store that night. It was a reasonable request, but they'd refused. He'd argued. They'd ignored his pleas. And then he'd shouted and thrown the joystick to the floor. That was why he'd been sent to bed early. And why his throat was sore. Before he fell asleep, his mind filled with wishes. Not all of them were nice.

Somna showed Michael how to speak a wish so it became a reality. As first, he had Michael wish for unimportant things—a pebble, a sheet of paper, a pencil, or a button.

Finally, Somna told Michael, "Wish for something of value."

"Anything?" Michael shivered as the possibilities flooded his mind.

"Start small," Somna said.

Michael wished for a joystick. It appeared on the bed. Then he wished for money. His hands filled with coins.

Some were from Earth. Others bore strange markings. Many seemed to be made of gold.

"This is awesome." As Michael counted his wealth, Somna drifted back into the shadows.

"Enjoy your harvest," the shadows whispered.

For a month, Michael worked on mastering his wishing skills. He learned to get exactly what he wanted. A wish for money, as he had seen, could bring all sorts of things. A wish for a crisp, new hundred-dollar bill brought exactly that. Not that he needed money, since he could just as easily wish for anything money could buy.

At midnight, a month later, on the next sliver beyond the new moon, Somna returned. "You have passed the trial period," he said. "Do you wish to become a full member of the League?"

"Of course," Michael said.

"Then your wish is granted." Somna brushed Michael's forehead with a claw. "You are one of us."

Michael felt as if a thread had been pulled from his mind and stretched across the universe. He tested his powers to make sure nothing had changed. The clink of coins filled the room as seventy-seven silver dollars fell on his blanket. That was exactly what he had wished for. He didn't need coins, but he liked owning them.

"Where does it come from?" Michael asked.

"The money?" Somna asked.

"Yeah."

"From others among the League. It is a closed universe. Nothing new is created. Objects move from place to place. Coins, cars, camels—it doesn't matter. It all has to come from somewhere."

"Okay." That was fine with Michael. He didn't mind wishing things away from other members. He didn't know them. And they didn't know him. It seemed like a perfect arrangement.

Somna turned to leave.

"Wait," Michael said as another thought cast a shadow across his joy. He scooped up a handful of the coins from the bed and clutched them in his fist. "Does that mean someone can take money from me?"

"They could," Somna said, "if any of them wanted something as useless as money. Most League members have other needs."

"Like what?" As Michael spoke, his shirt fell open. He glanced down and saw that all his buttons were missing.

"Whatever they want," Somna said.

"That's not fair. That's—" Michael's sentence ended with a yelp as he fell to the floor. For a moment, he couldn't figure out why he was no longer standing. When he tried to get back up, he saw the reason he'd lost his balance and toppled over. His left leg was missing.

"It looks like someone made a wish," Somna said.

Michael tried to scream, but his tongue and vocal cords were gone. He tried to wish them back, but part of his brain vanished, taking away his ability to think.

Other parts of Michael lasted a bit longer, but the League was large and had many needs. Soon, there was nothing left of Michael. Not even a wish.

THE DEPARTMENT STORE

So, we're thinking, maybe you're cool enough to hang out with us," Nicky said.

"Yeah." I was afraid to say much more. I didn't want to act too excited. But Nicky and his friends were awesome. They called themselves the Wolves because our school mascot was a mountain goat, and wolves could totally tear up any goat. They always took over the best basketball court at recess, and they had the coolest table at lunch. I couldn't believe they were actually giving me a chance to hang out with them.

"Of course, there's a little test," Nicky said.

"No problem." It didn't matter. I could handle anything.

"Let's see. . . ." Nicky turned toward the rest of the Wolves, who stood in a half circle near us at the edge of the ball field. "Any ideas?"

"Climb the old bell tower?" Stinky Miller suggested.

Nicky shook his head. "Nah, we don't want to lose this one. He'll probably make a good Wolf. Let's give him a break."

He paused for a moment, then snapped his fingers. "I know—all you have to do is spend the night in Brazzleberg's."

"You want me to spend the night in a store?" Brazzleberg's was an old department store downtown—four floors of stuff people used to buy before the mall came along. I'd heard that it was close to going out of business.

"Yeah, just hide when they lock up and spend the night there. That's all. Can you handle it?"

"No problem." It almost seemed too easy. Nobody shopped there anymore, and the people who still worked there didn't really care what happened.

"We'll need proof," Nicky said.

I thought for a second. I'm pretty smart, even if people don't treat me that way, so it was easy to think up something. "Come to the front entrance a half hour before they open. I'll be standing there waving at you."

Nicky grinned. "Cool. See you then." He punched me on the shoulder—his way of saying good-bye—and walked off. I waited for him to go back inside, then rubbed the spot where he'd hit me.

This was awesome. In less than a day I'd be the newest member of the Wolves. I went home and made up a couple sandwiches to take with me. I couldn't find any plastic bags, so I wrapped the sandwiches in newspaper and put them in my jacket pocket. Nobody asked what I was up to or when I'd be back. That was no surprise. As long as I didn't blow the place up or burn it down, they didn't really care what I did.

I walked to Brazzleberg's about a half hour before they closed. It was already growing dark by the time I got there. It wasn't that late, but a bunch of heavy clouds were coming in. I smiled at the thought of rain. It would be pretty funny if I was standing inside all warm and dry, waving to a bunch of wet Wolves getting soaked in a downpour. I'd have to be careful not to be too smug about it.

Nobody paid any attention to me when I walked inside the store. It was near closing time, so everybody was probably thinking about getting out of there and heading home. I took the elevator up to furniture department on the third floor. I found a bed that was covered with a long quilt. Perfect. I made sure no one was watching, then dropped down and rolled under the bed. Just like that, I was in. As I waited for the store to close, I listened to the sound of people walking by and the rumble of thunder in the distance.

Once, some little kid bounced on the bed. I thought about grabbing his ankle when he got off and giving him the scare of his life. It was almost too tempting to resist, but I managed to control myself. Still, it would have been fun to scare the little brat.

After a long, dark wait, I heard them announce that the store was closing. A while later, I peeked out to check. Most of the lights were off, except for some dim night-lights. I was alone. I rolled out from underneath the bed. This was going to be no trouble at all. I looked around for something to do. Across the aisle on one side I saw all kinds of pots and pans and other boring stuff. There was nothing except clothing on the other side.

I sat and ate a sandwich, then wandered over toward the clothes. There was one of those stupid mannequins near the aisle, wearing a fancy dress. "Pleased to meet you," I said. I reached out and shook her plaster hand.

A crash of thunder startled me. For an instant, the lights flickered off. For an instant I felt—no, it was too crazy. It couldn't have been. For that tiny fraction of a second when the light was out, the plaster hand I held seemed to become warm flesh. It was like when you put your hand on the ground and suddenly discover there's a worm underneath it.

I yanked my hand away. I reached to touch the mannequin again, just to make sure it was only plaster, then changed my mind and backed off. No use spooking myself.

The lights flickered again. I didn't like the idea that I could end up in the dark. I went over to the housewares section and snooped around. There was a package of candles. That would work. I searched a little more and found some lighters. I slipped one into my pocket and carried the candles back to the furniture department.

I returned to the bed, but kept an eye on the dozen mannequins in the clothing department. I didn't want to be too close to them, but I also didn't want them out of my sight.

The lights flickered again. They stayed off for only a couple heartbeats. That was enough.

She'd moved.

I couldn't say in what way, but she was different.

They all were.

I leaped off from the bed. Outside, the storm hit hard. Thunder shook the walls. The lights went out again. As the heartbeats stretched out far too long, I waited for the emergency lights to come on. They didn't.

I grabbed the candles. The box was wrapped in plastic. I tried to tear it, but I couldn't get it open. I heard something moving across the aisle.

I stumbled away, feeling ahead of myself in the dark. Footsteps shuffled behind me. It was dead black. The lighter! I grabbed it from my pocket and spun the wheel. The yellow-

and-blue flame put a circle of light around me, a shield against the night. The mannequins were frozen, gathered, facing me. I saw a clear aisle to my right that led all the way to the stairs. The lighter was getting hot in my hands. But I knew exactly which way to run, and how far.

I turned and raced down the aisle for the stairs, letting the flame die.

A dozen pairs of footsteps followed me. I found the banister with my free hand and ran down the steps, turning at each landing. I kept going until I reached the bottom. I flicked the light on again for an instant. A large aisle ran straight from the bottom of the stairs. There had to be a door ahead. I sped down the aisle, keeping my hand out in front of me to feel for the door.

I ran into a wall. The lighter fell from my fingers. I heard it bounce off the wall and slide across the linoleum. My hand, still pressed against the wall, told me what I didn't want to know. Instead of the glass of an exit door, I felt the rough, hard surface of painted cinder blocks. In my panic, I'd run past the ground floor, all the way down to the basement.

There were footsteps coming from the end of the aisle. They'd followed me.

I dropped to my knees and felt for the lighter. My fingers hit it. It slid. But I found it quickly. I flicked on the flame and looked behind me. The mannequins—at least a dozen of them—were halfway down the aisle from me. In the flickering light, they were nothing but lifeless plaster, bunched together like dead flowers forgotten in a vase.

I searched for a way out. The lighter was growing hot again. Then I saw my escape. I ran down the side aisle toward a sales counter.

They say I'm stupid. That's what they say in school. But a stupid kid wouldn't have figured out what to do. I reached the counter, then flicked on the lighter again to make sure. I jumped up on the counter. The ceilings were lower in the basement. I could reach the smoke detector. I wasn't stupid enough to think the lighter would set it off. I knew I needed smoke. But that was no problem. I pulled the second sandwich from my pocket, unwrapped it, lit the paper, and stood on my toes so I could hold the flaming paper close to the detector.

In seconds, the alarm would be triggered. The firemen would come and break through the door, shining flashlights in the dark store. I'd get in trouble—big trouble—but that was fine. I wasn't afraid of trouble.

A bell rang somewhere far off in the store. They must have a special power line for the alarms. I was smart enough to know that, too. Alarms always have their own power.

I could hold the mannequins off with the dim flame until I was rescued. I dropped the paper and stomped it out so I wouldn't get burned, but clutched the lighter in front of me with a shaking hand. The mannequins stood unmoving, unable to harm me in my circle of light.

Then the rain fell.

For an instant, as the water sprayed in my face from every direction, I had no idea why I was being soaked. I looked up just as the lighter died with a hiss. Water shot from a thousand sprinklers in the ceiling.

I thumbed the wheel. The wet flint wouldn't spark. I kept trying.

The footsteps came closer. I heard whispers, and then a laugh. Fingers wrapped around my ankle. I was yanked from the counter. A dozen pairs of hands grabbed my arms and legs.

"Pleased to meet you, too," a soft voice whispered.

"Join us," a second voice said.

"We have our own special club."

"We like you."

The Wolves gathered outside the store a half hour before opening time. The rain had stopped. Nicky was there, looking in the door. They were talking and laughing. I was just off to the side by the window. I waved to them. Well, I actually couldn't call it a wave. One hand was raised. I can't move when the lights are on. Maybe it's just as well they didn't notice me. I look kind of silly dressed in the jacket and tie. And I have this stupid smile stuck on my face. But that's all right. I'm with my new friends. I'll be with them forever. They really like me. Best of all, they know I'm not a dummy.

THE BATTLE OF THE RED
HOT PEPPER WEENIE*J*

It was the Battle of the Alamo all over again.

Let me back up a bit. This is about two kids in our school—Dallas Mitchell and Alonso Viejez. Dallas, as you might guess from his name, was born in Texas. He'd moved here from San Antonio last month. Alonso is from Mexico. He'd come here from Jalisco late last year.

Since they're both from the same hot and sunny part of the continent, and since they're living up here in cold, crisp Vermont, you might think they'd hang out together. But they pretty much ignored each other. Until last Tuesday at lunch.

Alonso was at our table, with me, Vin, Naveen, Dylan, and the rest of the guys. Dallas was right behind me at the next table, between Len and T.J. As Dallas was unwrapping his lunch, Len asked, "What are those?"

"Jalapeño slices," Dallas said. "But we pepper lovers call 'em Texas pickles. Try one."

I turned around and watched as Dallas slid a small container over to Len. Len took a slice of pepper and chewed on it. For about six seconds, nothing happened. Then Len's eyes opened wide. His mouth opened wider. His nostrils flared. I think his tonsils might have tried to leap from his throat. He screamed and raced for the water fountain down the hall by the boys' room.

"Bad move," Alonso said. "Water just makes it worse." Another scream from down the hall proved his point.

"Those must be pretty hot," I said. I like the sweet peppers they put on sandwiches, or the weird pale green ones I find in a salad once in a while, but I haven't had too much experience with jalapeños or other really hot stuff.

"They aren't hot if you're used to them," Alonso said.

I guess Dallas heard Alonso. He grinned, held up the container, and said, "Help yourself."

I figured Alonso would pick out a slice, like Len did. Instead, he took the container, tilted his head back, then dumped all the jalapeños into his mouth. He grinned, stared at Dallas, and slowly chewed the mouthful of green fire.

"Man, those guys are real pepper heads," Dylan said.

"More like Pepper Weenies," Naveen said. "You shouldn't mess with that stuff."

I waited. Six seconds passed. My own tongue burned in sympathy, but there was no sign Alonso was feeling anything. Finally, he opened his mouth again, not to scream or shoot flames, but to say, "Very mild Texas pickles, *amigo*. Maybe they'd be better with a dash of hot sauce?"

I guess there's nothing kids won't compete about—especially when it involves pain and suffering. On Wednesday, Alonso brought a couple of small bright orange peppers to lunch.

"I'm afraid to ask what those are," I said.

"Serranos," Alonso said. "Much hotter than jalapeños. Nobody will call these *pickles*." He said the last part loud enough to make sure Dallas heard him.

"Let me have one," Dallas said.

"Help yourself." Alonso tossed him a pepper.

Dallas bit into the serrano. From five feet away, I could feel my eyes burning. But Dallas just chewed, swallowed, and said, "Must be mild serranos." I think one drop of sweat might have rolled down his temple, but it was hard to see anything clearly at the moment.

On Thursday, Dallas held up a pepper and said, "Have a habañero, unless you think it's too hot for you."

"My pleasure." Alonso munched the pepper without flinching.

His eyes seemed to get moist, like my mom's do when she's cutting onions. I watched for tears, but all Alonso did was blink once.

Friday, it was Alonso's turn. "Red savinas," he said as he offered Dallas a handful of peppers. "They're like habañeros, but hotter."

"Good. I need something hot after that mild serrano of yours." Dallas ate the peppers like they were chocolate marshmallows.

Kids on either side of him started crying from the fumes. I noticed Dallas kept his mouth clamped tight after he finished chewing. His neck and jaw muscles trembled. I thought I heard a crack, like he broke a tooth. But his expression never changed.

"That's got to be the end of it," I said to Naveen after lunch. We'd had nearly a week of madness. "There can't be many kinds of pepper left."

"Maybe not from here," Naveen said. "But it's a big world out there. There's a pepper from India that's fifty times hotter than a jalapeño."

"Well, let's hope those guys don't find that out."

But on Monday, Dallas and Alonso both showed up at lunch with big grins and paper sacks stuffed full of peppers. They stood and faced each other. At the same time, they both thrust out their sacks and said, *"Bhut jolokia!"*

I glanced over at Naveen. "You didn't have anything to do with this, did you?"

He smiled and shrugged. "You think I'd tell those guys there's something out there that's too hot for them to handle?"

"I think you'd do exactly that," I said. "Have you ever eaten one of those?"

"Not a whole one. I might love peppers, but I'm not crazy. Those things would bring an elephant to its knees."

I turned my attention back to the battle. Dallas and Alonso stared at each other for a moment, like two gunfighters ready for a showdown. Then each grabbed the other's bag and popped a pepper.

"Stop," I said. "This is crazy." My eyes were burning, and my nose started running. I wiped my nose on my sleeve and saw scorch marks on my shirt.

They didn't pay any attention to me. They each ate a second pepper, and a third. Their faces got redder and redder. Their eyes filled with tears. Sweat streamed down their foreheads and washed over their cheeks. Their noses were dripping like tapped maple trees. I expected their teeth to melt and flow from their mouths. But they kept going. Neither of them would back down. Neither would stop chewing and swallowing.

I guess your tongue can get used to anything. But that's only the start of the trip the pepper has to make. Just as Dallas and Alonso were eating the last peppers, their bodies jerked like they'd suddenly realized they had something better—or, at least, more urgent—to do.

They turned and raced from the cafeteria. They ran right past the water fountain. I'm not sure, but I think I saw flames shooting out of the backs of their pants. Alonso was slightly ahead of Dallas, but they both got where they were going really quickly. They burst through the door of the boys' room and disappeared inside. I heard two stall doors slamming shut. I flinched as screams echoed down the hall. A smell that I can only describe as a sewer plant on fire drifted down the hall. Kids all around the cafeteria tossed away their lunches. Some tossed their cookies, too.

"Well, lunch should be more peaceful for a while," Naveen said.

He was right. The Pepper Weenies were out of school for a couple days. The next time I saw Alonso and Dallas, they each brought another paper sack to the cafeteria. Only, this time, the sacks contained cream cheese sandwiches on white bread.

JUST LIKE ME

Thanks. It's very nice," Deb said as she lifted the skirt from the box. She tried to sound pleased. It wasn't all that bad a skirt, but it was the sort of style she'd stopped wearing several years ago. Maybe she could exchange it for something she liked.

"You'll look so cute in it," her mom said. She pointed at the pile of empty boxes and smiled. "A present seems to be missing."

"Really?" Deb asked. That was more like it. Each birthday, she got one very special gift from her mom. So far, there'd been no sign of it.

"Stay right here. I've been saving the best for last." Her smile turned into a grin as she rushed out of the living room.

Deb wondered whether her mother had gotten her the portable DVD player she'd asked for. Or maybe it was her own television for her bedroom. Either would be great. She knew it would be unreasonable to hope for both.

A moment later, her mom returned with a package that

was about twice the size of a shoe box. Deb's hopes slowly deflated as she took the gift.

"Thanks." She shook it. Something solid clunked against the sides of the box. It didn't feel heavy enough for a DVD player, and it was too small to be a television.

"Careful," her mom said. "You'll hurt her."

Her? Deb removed the paper. Since this was the last present, she didn't want to rush. Once the presents were opened, she felt that the rest of the birthday was pretty much just like any other day.

Beneath the wrapping paper, she found a pink cardboard box. Curly white letters on the lid read, JUST LIKE ME.

Puzzled, Deb lifted the lid. Then she pulled aside the pink tissue paper that covered the contents. "Oh my . . ."

She found herself staring at her own face—smaller, hard, and unmoving, but still her own face, right down to the dark-brown bangs that covered her forehead and the light-brown freckles that dusted her cheeks. *Bangs?* Not anymore. Deb put a hand to her head. She'd changed her hairstyle nearly a year ago.

"Like it?" her mom asked.

Deb nodded, though she wasn't sure how she felt. She was too old for dolls. She'd packed all of hers away the last time she'd cleaned her room. Looking more closely, she realized the doll appeared sort of young.

"There's a man up in Glenville who makes them," her mom said. "He uses a photograph."

"Which picture did you send?" Deb asked.

"That wonderful shot from the summer before last. I think he did a fabulous job. It looks just like you."

"It's great, Mom." Deb picked up the doll, but she didn't

hold it too close. She felt strangely uncomfortable when she looked into the small version of her own face. It was like last year, when she'd been in the school play. The first time she'd seen her face in a mirror wearing stage makeup, the sight had made her feel weird. Everything was familiar, but also slightly odd.

"I knew you'd be thrilled," her mom said. "I couldn't wait to give her to you."

Deb carried the doll up to her room and looked for a place to put it. She couldn't bring herself to give the thing a name. What could she call it? Little Deb? Deb the Second? Young Deb? No. For now, the doll was an *it*. But she needed a place for it. Deb knew her mom would be hurt if she stuck the doll in a closet. Or in the trash. She settled for putting it on the shelf that ran along the wall above her headboard. That way, at least, she wouldn't see the doll when she was lying in bed.

Before she went to sleep, she checked online. The company that made the doll had a Web site. To her horror, she discovered the doll cost more than a DVD player and a TV put together. *What a waste*, she thought as she got in bed.

When Deb woke up the next morning, she felt something hard next to her head. She reached out, her eyes still closed, and touched cold plastic. Wiry hair brushed against her fingertips. Deb sat up fast, letting out a gasp.

The doll was in bed with her. *It must have fallen*, Deb thought as she scooted away from it. But that wouldn't explain how the doll had ended up tucked under the blanket next to her. Deb didn't want to think about that. She put the doll back on the shelf and went down for breakfast.

"Could you get the paper?" her mom asked when Deb walked into the kitchen.

"Sure." Deb threw on her coat and went out to the front lawn.

When she got back to the kitchen, she nearly dropped the paper. The doll was sitting at the kitchen table, perched in a chair, boosted by a stack of books.

"I thought she should join us," Deb's mom said.

Deb nodded and took a seat. She noticed her mom had set a place for the doll.

"So," her mom said, "have you given her a name yet?"

"No," Deb said. "I'm still thinking about it."

"How about Anne?"

"But . . . ," Deb said. *Anne* was her own middle name. Her dad had come up with Deb. Her mom had come up with Anne. So they'd named her Deborah Anne.

Her mom stroked the doll's hair. "Yes. Anne. I like that. Don't you?"

"Sure, Mom," Deb said. "Anne is a great name." She glanced up at the clock. "I'd better get going." She grabbed her backpack and hurried down the hall toward the front door. As she looked over her shoulder, she saw Anne sitting at the table, staring with eyes that never moved, waiting patiently for someone to pick her up or stroke her hair and tell her what a good girl she was.

When Deb got home from school, she found Anne on the couch. Deb always sat on the left corner of the couch to do her homework. Her mom had put Anne in her spot. Deb carried the doll to the other side of the room and dropped her onto the large leather chair her dad had loved to lounge in—the chair he'd always sat in before he'd left last year.

Deb sat on the couch and started her homework. A few minutes later, she heard her mom coming down the hall.

She realized her mom would want to know why she'd moved Anne. Deb ran over and brought Anne back to the couch, placing her on the middle cushion.

"Oh, don't the two of you look cute," Deb's mom said. She walked over to the couch and gave Deb a hug. Then she reached down and patted Anne. "What an adorable pair." She raised her other hand, which held a brush, and started brushing Anne's hair.

"We're not a pair," Deb muttered. Her own scalp tingled as she spoke. She turned away from the doll and continued working on her homework, trying to ignore the tuneless drone of her mother's humming.

Anne joined the family for dinner that night. Once again, Deb's mom set a plate for the doll. *At least she didn't give her any food*, Deb thought as she ate her meal.

That evening, after the three of them watched television, Deb's mom stood up and said, "Bedtime, Deborah Anne."

Deb was about to answer when she realized that her mom was talking to the doll. *Deborah Anne?* Deb thought. It must have been a slip. A stupid slip. "Fine," she muttered as she went upstairs to get ready for bed. "If that's what she wants. Just fine. They can have each other."

She stomped down the hall to the bathroom. When she finished brushing her teeth, she walked into her room.

Anne was sitting on her bed. Deb froze in the doorway. Down the hall, she could hear her mom in her own bedroom. "I'll be there in a minute to say good night," her mom called.

Deb sat at the foot of the bed, far from Anne. Her mother came in and said good night to them, looking straight at the doll the whole time. As soon as her mom left, Deb tossed

Anne up onto her shelf. Hard. She smiled at the sound of the doll's head smacking against the wall.

Sleep tight, Deb thought as she crawled under the covers.

Deb woke in the middle of the night with a headache. She knew, without checking, that Anne was tucked in next to her again. Deb closed her eyes, curled up with her back to the doll, and tried to sleep.

The next day, after school, Deb had an idea. She'd fix things so Anne didn't look like her anymore. Then her mother would snap out of this weirdness. "Shock her right out of it," Deb said as she went to the kitchen and grabbed a knife.

"Plastic surgery," she muttered. "A little off the nose. A little off the cheeks. A whole new face." She was halfway to the couch when her mom's scream locked her in her tracks.

"What are you doing?" her mom asked, pointing at the knife.

Deb shrugged and spat out the first lie that came to mind. "Nothing. I was just going to trim her hair. The bangs are too long."

"With that? Have you lost her mind?" Her mom snatched the doll from the couch and wrapped her arms tightly around it, cradling the doll against her chest. "There, there," she crooned. "It's all right."

Deb turned away and went back to the kitchen. Her chest felt so tight, she could hardly breathe. She put the knife back in the drawer, then sat at the table.

A while later, she heard steps.

"Deborah Anne forgives you," her mom said. "She's very understanding. Everyone says she's a perfect doll."

Deb nodded, but didn't look up at them. She heard her

mom put the doll on a chair. Her own breath came more easily now.

"I don't want her in my room tonight," Deb said.

"Sure you do," her mother said. "Besides—it's her room, too."

"No, it isn't!" Deb shot up from the chair and leaned toward her mom. "It's my room. She's a doll! She isn't real!"

Her mom reached out and placed her hands over the doll's ears. "Ssshhhhh. I don't know what's come over you."

Deb stormed out of the house. She walked aimlessly for blocks, dreaming of how she was going to destroy the doll. The house was dark when she got home. Her mother had gone to bed. *She didn't even wait up for me*, Deb thought.

Upstairs, in her room, the doll waited for her. It was on her bed, tucked under the blanket. Deb's favorite bracelet was fastened around the doll's neck. Her mom must have put it there.

"Enough!" Deb said. She raced across the room and grabbed the doll. She fumbled with the catch on the bracelet, then stopped. She was afraid that she'd break the chain. There was an easier way to get it off. A much more satisfying way. She twisted the doll's head, eager to rip it right off the body. In her mind, she saw herself throwing the head through her window. In her mind, she saw herself screaming at her mother, telling her how wrong all of this was. In her mind, she saw the world returning to the way it once had been.

In her neck, she felt a slash of tearing pain that hurt beyond anything she could imagine.

The doll dropped from her fingers and fell to the bed. Deb staggered back, grabbing her injured throat. She crashed into the wall, then sank to the floor. A weak gasp came from her lips. She couldn't raise her voice above a whisper, or turn her head to the front. On the bed, she saw the doll, its head twisted at an unnatural angle.

"Deb!" her mother cried, racing into the room.

Deb reached out a hand and mouthed the word "Neck."

Her mother sped past her. She grabbed the doll and cradled it in her arms. "Yes, your poor neck. How awful. Oh, dear. Don't worry, I'll get you taken care of. You'll be fine. You'll be just fine, Deborah Anne. I promise."

She rushed from the room, still talking to the doll. "Don't worry. I know someone who can fix you. She lives right across town."

Deb, struggling to swallow, watched her go. A half hour later, as she sat on the floor in a corner of her room, her neck suddenly felt better. She knew the doll had been repaired.

Her mom would be back soon. Her mom and Deborah Anne. Perfect Deborah Anne who never disobeyed. Who never sulked or pouted. Who never grew older. "No," she said aloud. "I'm Deb. She's just a doll. I'm Deb. Not her. Me."

But even to her own ears, her voice sounded flat and empty. Not human, really. Not very much alive at all.

WHAT'S EATING
THE VEGANS?

I love Thanksgiving. Or, at least, I did until about half an hour ago. That's when my cousin Krystal and her family showed up. She's a lot older than I am, and has a husband and two gooey little kids. They were passing through Pennsylvania today on their way down to Florida, so Mom and Dad invited them to join us for dinner. On Thanksgiving. Which is the absolute worst day in the world to sit down at a table with vegans.

I hadn't even known that word before today. Here's how I learned it. Right after Cousin Krystal and her family came through the door, she handed Mom a big box wrapped in foil. "I brought a tofurkey," she said.

"What's that?" I asked. It almost sounded like a bad word.

"A tofu turkey," she said. "We're vegans. We don't eat meat or fish or milk or eggs."

"Meat is murder," her daughter, Aggy, said.

"Meat is tasty," I said.

"Now, Eric, you need to respect other people's beliefs," Mom said.

And they don't have to respect mine? I kept my mouth shut.

Mom put the tofurkey in the oven. I helped set the table. Aggy and her little brother, Sam, followed me around. "Do you have any companion animals?" he asked.

"What?" I didn't have a clue.

They both looked at me like I was stupid, then said, "Dogs or cats?"

"You mean pets?" I asked.

"That's what unethical barbarians call them," Aggy said. "Civilized people call them companions."

"Yeah. I've got a companion. He lives in a bowl of water in my bedroom. He stinks at keeping me company because every time I take him out of the water so we can do stuff together, he starts to die." I did an imitation of a gasping fish. I think it was pretty good. My second cousins thought otherwise.

"Mom!" Aggy shouted, "Cousin Eric is being mean."

"You stink," Sam said. "Fish killer."

Mom shot me a glare wrapped in a long sigh, which I knew was a dangerous combination. But I could tell that Dad was struggling not to laugh.

The real food was ready, so we sat down at the table. "Happy Thanksgiving," Dad said. He put the turkey on the table and picked up the carving knife. The bird was a beauty. Twelve pounds, fat and juicy. And it came from the local turkey farm, right across the river. I couldn't wait to bite into a drumstick. At least I wouldn't have to fight my second cousins for one.

"Happy turkey slaughter day," Aggy said.

I turned toward her and made a slashing motion with my knife. "I'm pretty sure most of the turkeys were slaughtered a couple days ago."

"*Mom!*" Aggy shouted. "Make him stop!"

My mom shot me another glare. I shut up. But Cousin Krystal kept lecturing us. "Meat is ruining the whole planet. They put all sorts of hormones in cattle feed. And all that stuff washes into the rivers and pollutes everything. It's a miracle there aren't giant fish or something flopping on the banks. On top of which, you're two miles from a nuclear re-actor, and less than three miles from a pesticide plant. It's amazing you all aren't mutants or giants."

"Or giant mutants," I muttered, just loudly enough for Dad to hear.

"Meat pollutes your whole body," Cousin Krystal said.

"Vegans are healthier," Aggy said. "We make better ath-letes. I'll bet I can run faster than you."

"Mmmmmm, nice thick gravy." I licked my lips. "Some things aren't meant to run. Like gravy."

After I finished the drumstick, which I purposely chewed with my mouth open while staring at Aggy, I got a slab of white meat and drowned it in gravy.

"Animals have feelings, too," Cousin Krystal said.

"This one feels crispy," I muttered. I kept my voice down, but Dad flashed me a smile. He loves steak.

I was just helping myself to thirds when the side of the house crashed in. I heard the loudest gobbling sound in the world, and a giant turkey burst into the dining room. It was so tall, its comb touched the ceiling.

"Run!" Dad shouted.

We all scrambled outside through the opening in the wall. The turkey in our house wasn't alone. I could see sev-eral more giant turkeys making their way across the river from the turkey farm.

We raced out of our yard and headed up the hill behind the house. I was feeling a bit sluggish from all that food. Aggy hadn't exaggerated about her foot speed. She and the rest of the vegans got way ahead of us. As Cousin Krystal reached the top of the hill, she paused long enough to taunt me. "See? Meat will get you killed. You pathetic carnivore."

She might be right. The turkeys were catching up with us.

"At least my last meal tasted good!" I shouted as I tried for a final, desperate burst of speed. I stumbled and fell. I was too stuffed to get up.

Seconds later, one of the turkeys hovered over me. It pecked at my leg, sending a jolt of agony through my thigh. I braced myself for another peck, but the turkey paused and cocked its head, as if thinking. Instead of attacking me, it did something I didn't know birds could do. It spat. Then it shuddered, gobbled some giant turkey sounds at its giant turkey friends, and raced past us meat eaters, heading up the hill toward the vegans.

"I hope they don't like the taste of vegans, either," I said. As much as I didn't want to have another meal with the vegans, I didn't really want them to become a meal, either.

The shrieks that came from the other side of the hill a couple moments later told me I hadn't gotten my wish. So, while these particular turkeys aren't vegans themselves, it turns out that, unlike me, they like having vegans for dinner. Go figure.

Mom got up and dusted herself off. "There's pie," she said.

"Sounds good," Dad said. "And we can have sandwiches later. There are plenty of leftovers. That was one large bird you cooked for us this year."

"I've seen bigger," I said.

Dad grinned at me. "I guess we'll always be able to say that."

Mom and Dad headed down the hill. I followed. Dad was right. Pie sounded good.

LET'S HAVE A BIG
HAND FOR GERALD

The first sign was the left glove. Gerald tugged at it and managed to get it on. But it felt tight. The right one had slipped over his hand with no trouble.

"Mom, my glove is tight," he called.

"It probably shrank when it got wet," she called back from the living room. "It's leather. It'll stretch."

But the glove didn't stretch. The next day, Gerald looked for his old gloves. They were wool. Wool definitely stretched.

The second sign, a week or so later, appeared when Gerald was washing his hands. This happened rarely enough, but he'd gotten ketchup on them while he was eating his fries. As he rubbed them together under the water, he noticed that the left hand definitely seemed larger.

"Mom," he called, "my left hand is bigger than my right hand."

"People aren't perfectly symmetrical," she called back.

Gerald wasn't sure what that meant. He dried his hands, put on his right glove, forced on his left glove, which stretched so much, he could see his skin through the knitted wool, and tried to put on his jacket. But his left hand wouldn't fit through the sleeve.

"Mom," he called. "My jacket doesn't fit."

"People grow," she called. "Look in the closet for another one."

Gerald searched through the closet. He found a coat with bigger sleeves. It hung way past his knees, but he didn't care.

A month later, that coat didn't fit, either, but the weather had grown warm enough so he could get by with just a sweater—which wasn't too hard to tug on.

Soon after that, Gerald realized he had to stop putting anything in his left pants pocket because there was no way he could reach in to take stuff out.

His left hand was a lot bigger than his right. A month or so later, this became a real problem.

"Mom. I can't get any of my shirts on," he called.

"It's warm enough to go shirtless!" she yelled back.

So he did. Eventually, his fingertips started to bleed. Gerald realized they were scraping the ground when he walked. He found his old wagon and put his hand in it. That was better. But even with the wagon, his shoulder was starting to ache all the time.

He went inside. "Mom, can you look at my hand?"

"Stop being such a baby," she called back.

"Please?"

"Oh, come in then," she said. "But hurry up. The commercial's almost over."

Gerald walked down the hall to the living room. He went through the doorway and squeezed past the gigantic left foot that was propped on a stool near the couch.

"What's the problem?" his mom asked. She didn't look away from the television.

"Nothing," Gerald said. Sighing, he dragged his hand back into the hallway.

BIRD SHOT

I think summer camp was invented by the same person who dreamed up opera. There's no reason for it to exist, nobody except grown-ups thinks it's a good idea, and it can cause an extreme amount of misery for everyone involved.

So there I was, unpacking my clothes in cabin five at Camp Wamaguchi. Right after I jammed the last of my T-shirts into the locker and tossed out the vitamins Mom had packed for me, the kid at the end of the row waved me toward his bunk. He was a heavy kid—but not really fat—with a bad haircut and a nice shirt. I noticed he chewed his fingernails.

"Come here," he whispered. He glanced around like he was making sure none of the counselors was nearby.

I could have said, *No, you come here.* Or I could have ignored him. But I went. There's no point making enemies on the first day. "What?"

"Check it out." He leaned down and slid something out from under his bunk. It was a blanket. Actually, something wrapped in a blanket. He pulled back a corner. I saw brass and wood. Now he had my interest.

"BB gun? I asked.

"Yup." He dropped the blanket back in place, slid the gun back under his bed, and winked at me. "We're going to have some fun this summer."

A minute later, we all got called outside so we could meet one another. The kid's name was Elton. I noticed he didn't participate all that much in any of the activities. Mostly, he hung back and kept looking at our cabin.

That evening, after dinner, when we were supposed to be reading quietly and not bothering the counselors, Elton said, "I'm going shooting. Want to come?"

"Sure." My cousin had a BB pistol. I liked plinking at cans and stuff. I followed Elton outside. We snuck along the path away from the counselors' cabins and followed the trail downhill to a large clearing.

Elton finally stopped in the center of the clearing. "There's one." He pumped the lever, raised the BB gun, and fired off a shot.

I followed the line from the muzzle to the sky and saw a bird about twenty yards away.

"Not cool," I said. "You shouldn't shoot at birds."

"It doesn't hurt them," Elton said. "It's just a little BB."

He spun away from me and shot at another bird. This one was closer. I thought I saw it startle, but it kept flying and didn't seem to be injured.

"Want a shot?" he asked, holding out the BB gun.

"No, thanks."

"Chicken?"

"Not me." I grabbed the gun, pumped it, and waited to spot a bird. They weren't hard to find. They were heading to their nests to settle down for the evening. When I saw one, I aimed a bit low before I fired.

"I think you missed," Elton said.

"I'm not much of a shot."

"Stick with me," he said. "I never miss."

I stuck with him until he was done, but promised myself I'd make an excuse the next time he wanted to go out. I really didn't think it was fun to shoot at animals. I mean, hunting was one thing. I had relatives who hunted. But this wasn't hunting. It was something sick and evil, and it told me as much as I needed to know about Elton.

He invited me out again the next evening, but I said I had to write some letters. I found another excuse the day after that. Elton just shook his head and said, "You're no fun." I figured that was the end of it.

I saw my first dead bird at the start of the second week. I was out near the clearing, looking for arrowheads. The bird was lying at the edge of the woods, dark and ruffled. I couldn't say for sure that it had been killed by a BB, and I wasn't about to conduct an autopsy, but the sight didn't make me feel very good.

I saw three more dead birds in the next two days. And a dead squirrel that had been shot in the eye. Finally, I forced myself to do something I really didn't want to do. I told a counselor that Elton had a BB gun under his bed. I watched from the doorway as the counselor stormed into the cabin and reached under the bed. He slid the blanket out and dropped it on the mattress.

Elton sat there, not saying anything. He seemed weirdly calm for someone who was about to get in a ton of trouble.

The counselor unfolded the blanket, revealing a two-piece fishing rod.

"Sorry to bother you," the counselor said. He glared at me as he left the cabin.

Elton flashed me a smile, then went back to his magazine. I figured he'd jump me later, when it got dark. But I made it through the night without trouble.

The next afternoon, when I was swimming in the lake, I felt a sudden sting on my cheek. I dove underwater, figuring it was a bee. But when I came up, I spotted Elton on the far bank. He was holding something behind his back. Then he walked into the woods. I touched my cheek. There was a small round hole—not deep enough to draw blood, but deep enough to sting.

I got shot a couple more times that week. I would have put up with it, maybe, except I also stumbled across a whole cluster of dead birds.

I needed to stand up for the animals. Elton must have hidden his BB gun in the woods. That much, I'd figured out. I'd just have to follow him tonight and see where he kept it. Then I could break it or jam it somehow, so he wouldn't be able to use it again.

After he slipped out of the cabin that evening, I followed him. "You'll be safe soon," I whispered, looking up at the birds overhead. I knew that was stupid. But I felt like I was here to protect them.

There were more birds overhead than usual. I saw a steady stream of them flapping toward us from all directions. There was something odd about the way they were flying, but I couldn't tell for sure what the difference was. Maybe they'd all been injured. That thought gave me the courage to do whatever it took to stop Elton.

He crossed the clearing and entered the woods on the far side. He kept going until he reached a smaller clearing. There were birds all over, circling in the air and swooping across the sky.

I moved closer, but stayed out of sight behind a tree. Elton reached under a bush and pulled out the BB gun. As he raised the gun, I thought about tackling him. Even though he outweighed me, I was pretty sure I could take him in a fair fight. But I had the feeling he was a dirty fighter. He'd probably hit me with the butt of the gun. This would be better. I could wait, and then break the gun after he left.

My fists clenched in anticipation of his first shot. But before Elton could pull the trigger, he said, "Ouch!" and slapped a hand on top of his head. He put the hand back on the trigger and looked around, like he was puzzled about something. Then he shrugged and raised the gun to his shoulder again.

"Ouch!" This time, he dropped the gun and looked up. I still had no idea what was going on. But I heard the next one. I guess it hit his forehead. There was a definite plunk. Elton jerked, grabbed his head, and hunched over.

Above us, the birds chirped and swooped. I heard a couple more isolated thumps, and then a steady cascade of taps and clunks as the birds dropped their rocks. Pebbles and small stones rained from the sky.

I took a couple steps toward Elton, thinking maybe I could lead him back to the shelter of the woods. But one hit from a plummeting stone on my knuckles was enough to make me change my mind.

Elton staggered toward the trees, but the bigger birds had shown up by now, with bigger rocks. They dove toward him before releasing their loads, striking him at an angle and forcing him back to the middle of the clearing.

I didn't want to see this part. Eager to move beyond the sound of striking stones, I made my way back toward camp. I guess out here, deep in the woods, Nature sometimes finds a way to deal with human nature.

THE PRINCE$$ AND
THE PEA BRAIN

Once, there was a prince who was less than perfect. Far, far less than perfect. His parents, the king and queen, worried that he would suffer some terrible fate if he didn't have a princess to look after him when the time came for him to rule the kingdom.

"You need to find a wife," the queen told the prince.

So the prince went off to search for the perfect princess. He traveled throughout the realm and met many beautiful young ladies, but none of them seemed quite right for him. Not only was he somewhat dim-witted, but he was also far too picky. So he returned to his castle without a bride.

A month later, a terrible storm blew across the land. As the wind and rain beat at the walls, a beautiful young lady entered the castle, drenched and dripping. Her clothes, as wet as they were, seemed to be those of royalty. Her posture and charm also spoke of royal blood.

"Are you a princess?" the queen asked.

"Yes, I am," the princess said. "Though I have lost my

home and have wandered far in search of a place where I can belong."

The king and queen exchanged meaningful glances. "This might work," the queen whispered to the king.

"As long as she's a real princess," the king whispered back. "We can't let the prince marry a commoner."

"We can test that," the queen said, for she was wise in the ways of royalty, and had once been a princess herself.

The queen told the princess, "You must be exhausted. I'll have a room prepared for you, with a comfortable bed and a warm fire."

The princess curtsied, for she had perfect manners. The queen found the prince and took him to the royal guest room. "Get a pea from the kitchen. A single pea. Place a pea on the mattress. And then place another ten mattresses on top of the pea." She made sure to explain each step carefully, since the prince had been known to become easily confused. "We'll see how well the princess sleeps."

The queen went off and led the princess the long way through the castle, giving the prince plenty of time to place the pea and the mattresses on the bed. The queen hoped that, for once in his life, the prince paid careful attention to her instructions.

All night, the princess tossed and turned atop the pile of mattresses. She felt as if she was sleeping on a large round rock.

"How did you sleep?" the queen asked her in the morning.

"I didn't sleep," the princess said. "There was a lump in my mattress. It was as hard as a boulder."

The queen squealed in delight and ran off to find the

prince. But the prince was nowhere to be found. The queen had everyone search the castle.

Finally, someone noticed a foot sticking out from the other side of the bed. They found the prince beneath ten mattresses.

"It appears he crawled under there with a pea in his hand, and got trapped," the royal coroner said. "Though I can't imagine why he'd do something that foolish."

"That explains the lump," the princess said, rubbing her stiff back with her hands. "And the way the bed seemed to shake for a while. I'd thought there might be an earthquake. But then things settled down."

"So we still don't know if she's really a princess," the queen said. "Anyone would have felt that lump."

"I suppose it doesn't really matter," the king said, "since we have no prince for her to marry."

"But you still have a kingdom that will need a ruler," the princess said. "And I need a kingdom to rule."

"Then it is settled," the king said, for he knew when he was getting a good deal.

And so they all lived happily ever after. Except for the pea-brained prince, of course, who died horribly, ever earlier.

PETRO-FIED

I heard the growl from next door while we were sitting at the dinner table. It sounded like a prehistoric beast. I could even feel the slightest bit of vibration where my feet rested on the floor. Mr. Swinkle must have just pulled into his driveway.

Dad glanced over, too. "What a waste," he muttered.

"Totally." I had to agree with him. Mr. Swinkle's car, a brand-new Humongo V12, couldn't possibly get more than three or four miles to the gallon. And he was proud of that.

As the engine shut off, I heard three doors slam, followed by the high-pitched squeals of Effie and Steffie, Mr. Swinkle's unbearably snobby daughters, who were little gas guzzlers in training.

The Swinkles had moved here last year, and they immediately started adding stuff to their house. They expanded the garage so it could hold three cars and a boat. They put in a heated pool, which they ran all year round. I can't even imagine how much energy they burned keeping the water warm through the Pennsylvania winter. Even now, in April,

I could see steam rising from the pool when Dad drove me to school each morning.

Mr. Swinkle owned more gas-powered stuff than anyone—a riding mower, a walking mower, a leaf blower, a snowblower, a weed trimmer, a hedge trimmer so big it could be used to slay a dragon, and a boat with not one but two enormous outboard engines. Effie and Steffie each had go karts, minibikes, and ATVs. They'd probably get gas-powered flamethrowers when they turned eighteen. I'm surprised the Swinkles didn't have their own gas pump.

We'd learned about conservation in science class, and about how important it is not to waste energy or natural resources. I guess some people just didn't get the message. Mom and Dad sure did. They drive a hybrid car. Dad drops Mom off at her job on the way to his so we only need one car. And we put low-energy bulbs in all our lamps. I hope we're doing enough to make up for people like Mr. Swinkle.

That night, Dad said, "Do you mind walking to school tomorrow? I have to go to work early."

"No problem." It was a long walk, but I could usually count on running into a friend on the way there, so I didn't mind. Before Dad left, I asked him, "Are we going to run out of oil?"

"Not for a while," he said.

"But the fields here ran out." The first oil wells in the country were in Pennsylvania, not far from where we lived. But there aren't any working ones left. They got all of the oil out of the ground, and then went off to other states.

"That's why we need smart kids like you," Dad said. "So you can find other sources of energy. Believe it or not, before people drilled wells, most of the country's oil came from whales. Now it comes from dead dinosaurs and prehistoric plants. Actually, it's more complicated than that. But you're right—it won't last forever." He ruffled my hair. "So start thinking of other ways to power our cars and that video game you spend so much time playing."

I hoped it wasn't up to me. I didn't feel all that smart. I was a lot better at gym than at science. Even if I didn't have any answers, I guess the problem stayed in my mind because, that night, I dreamed Mr. Swinkle was draining my blood to fill his tank. The ghosts of a billion whales drifted past me.

The next morning, thunder woke me before my alarm went off. "Oh, great," I said when I heard the rain slamming against the side of the house. It looked like I was in for a wet walk.

I kept hoping the rain would slack off, but as I ate my breakfast, the water just seemed to come down harder and harder. When I stepped off the porch, it was like wading into the ocean. As I headed down the sidewalk, I saw Mr. Swinkle backing his Humongo out of his driveway. The roof of the car, pounded by the rain, sounded like a steel drum.

Mr. Swinkle pulled over to the curb. "Hop in, Dominic. I'll give you a ride."

Oh, man. I didn't know what to do. I was going to drown if I walked. But if I took a ride from him, that was almost the same as saying it was okay to drive around in a car that sucked gas like a sponge and spewed fumes like a volcano.

"Come on, you're getting wet."

I guess, since he was going there anyhow, it wasn't all that bad for me to get inside. Effie and Steffie were in the backseat, watching two different movies on the video screens that dropped down from above. There was still enough space next to them to fit five more kids, a small horse, and a couple motorcycles.

Mr. Swinkle pointed to the front passenger seat. I walked around, opened the door, and climbed up. The seat must have been eight feet off the ground. The inside of the car was larger than my room.

"Thanks," I said. Even if I hated his car, there was no reason not to be polite.

"No problem."

He drove on through the rain. Behind me, the girls chattered with each other. I couldn't help it. I had to ask him something. "Aren't you worried we'll run out of oil?"

He laughed. "Not in my lifetime. There's plenty to take me where I want to go."

I glanced over my shoulder. *What about your kids?* But I didn't ask. I figured he'd just make fun of me.

My attention shot toward the windshield as Mr. Swinkle slammed on the brakes. A large tree blocked the road ahead of us. "Yay," Effie shouted. "We can't go to school."

"Sure you can," Mr. Swinkle said. "That's why I bought this baby. She'll go anywhere." He cranked the steering wheel hard, and drove up the hill on our right.

"Do you know where you're going?" I asked. I could barely see anything now, but I could hear tree branches swiping at the sides of the car.

"Don't have to know." He tapped a screen on the dashboard. "Got a GPS to tell me where to go."

A voice from the dashboard said, "Recalculating route." Above the screen, I could swear I saw the gas gauge slowly moving. The Humongo had an endless thirst.

We went uphill for a while, and then down. And then

across a field. When the rain slowed for a moment, I saw something towering in the distance. It was the remains of one of the old oil wells.

"Turn left," I said. I knew exactly where we were. If we headed left for half a mile, we'd come out right on Bear Creek Road, just a couple hundred yards away from the turn for the school.

Mr. Swinkle pointed to the GPS. "Nope. We need to go straight. You can't outthink technology."

"But . . ."

He didn't even look at me. He just kept driving. A strong gust of wind blew the rain off the windshield for an instant. I saw something else up ahead. Something larger than the rusty remains of the oil wells.

I shook my head and blinked my eyes. It couldn't be. I stared, and waited for another glimpse.

Yeah. It was there. No mistake. The Humongo slowed down as we crossed a muddy stretch of field.

"You know what. I think I can walk from here." I wrapped my fingers around the door handle and prepared to argue with him. No responsible adult would let a kid out in the middle of a field in a major thunderstorm.

Mr. Swinkle shrugged. "Suit yourself."

I felt the car roll to a stop. *Am I sure?* I stared through the window again. The rain blurred the view, but I was sure. I stepped into the full fury of the storm and headed in the direction of the school. I wanted to get as far from the Humongo, and the people who rode in it, as possible. Rain and wind tore at my body. Mud dragged at my feet.

The car drove off. Fear fought with curiosity. I needed to know what would happen. I turned to watch. Ahead, near one of the wells, I saw what was waiting. They were huge. Even though they were transparent, the sight was enough to make me drop to my knees. My pants got soaked, but I didn't care. I was hypnotized by the magnificence and size of the creatures.

All three of them moved toward the Humongo. They were unbelievably graceful, despite their size. They seemed to grow more solid with each step. Soon, I could no longer see through them.

The first—I think it was an apatosaurus—reached the car ahead of the others. It raised its left front leg and placed its massive foot on the hood of the Humongo. The tires kept turning, spraying mud, but the car stopped.

The second dinosaur, a triceratops, moved in from one side and placed its horns against the roof. I couldn't identify the third, but it looked like a carnivore. It strode up behind the Humongo. Then all three of them pressed down on it. I heard the tires spin for another moment, then stop as the rims moved below the mud.

Once, oil had oozed from the ground here. Now, a car sank down. The whole Humongo disappeared beneath the surface.

The three dinosaurs lumbered off toward the wells, fading as they moved. I watched until they were totally swallowed by the rain and by the past. Then I turned and headed to school. Along the way, I thought about energy and oil and the future.

I got to school late and wet. But I got there. From that day on, I never flipped a light switch or got in a car without thinking about those ghosts.

TIME OUT

Maxwell's dad is a genius. Maxwell's my buddy. His dad was out in Sweden getting some kind of important science prize. Maxwell and I were down in the basement, where his dad had a workshop. "Is this what he got the prize for?" I asked, pointing to a large box that was covered with all kinds of dials and buttons.

"Nope," Maxwell said, shaking his head. "Nobody knows about this yet. It's a secret."

"What is it?" I walked over and took a closer look at Maxwell's dad's secret. There was a big switch on the left side that said ON/OFF. I flipped it to the ON position. The machine hummed like a copier warming up.

"Hey, don't fool with that," Maxwell said. But he didn't flip it off.

"Well, what is it?" There was a panel in the front, like the display on a microwave. The number 00:00 was flashing.

"Promise you won't tell anyone?"

"I promise." Next to the display, I noticed a keypad with numbers and other symbols.

"It's a time machine," Maxwell said.

"Cool. Let's go somewhere." I pushed one of the keys. The display now read 00:05.

"We can't. I'll get in trouble."

"Come on—your dad's in Sweden. Your mom's shopping for groceries with my mom. What can happen?"

There were two larger keys. One said FORWARD. The other said BACKWARD. I pushed BACKWARD. The display now showed −00:05. I figured it was either five seconds or five minutes. Either way, whatever happened would be interesting.

"Please," Maxwell said. But I could tell he really wanted me to do it.

I reached for a button that said ACTIVATE. Just as I was pushing the button, I heard a shout. *"No! Stop!"* I glanced at Maxwell. He hadn't said anything. Before I could figure out who was shouting at me, the machine made this loud hiss, like the sound a can of coffee makes when you open it.

Everything went sort of fuzzy and I felt myself flying through the air. I shot backwards and landed on the couch.

Wow. That was quite a jolt. It took me a couple of seconds to shake it off. Then I looked up and froze. Maxwell was standing next to the time machine. So was I. I mean, I was on the couch, but I saw myself standing by the machine, too. I'd gone back five seconds, to before I pushed the button. There were two of me. No, there were three of me, I realized. Another me—the one who had shouted the first warning— was right next to me on the couch. And I was about to press the button again.

I had to stop me. *"No! Stop!"*

My other me ignored my shout. I—I mean he—pushed the button.

He shot through the air toward the couch. I dove out of the way. I just missed getting clobbered as he hit the spot where I'd been sitting. I guess, being him, I got dragged back through time again, too. When I looked over, I was also standing at the machine. The me who landed on the couch shouted, *"No! Stop!"* The me at the machine hit the button.

The room was filling up at a steady rate. Another me hit the couch every five seconds. It's a good thing my mom went out for groceries. She's going to have a lot of kids to feed.

GALACTIC ZAP

Jimmy only had a quarter. Even so, he walked to the arcade. It was better than sitting around at home bored out of his mind. When he reached the arcade, he realized he was out of luck. All the cool games cost fifty cents or more. Then he noticed one, shoved in a far corner. Galactic Zap. It looked pretty old. But right on the coin slot, he saw a big blue *25*. He walked over to it, then hesitated, reluctant to make a bad decision.

"Is this any good?" he said out loud in the general direction of a cluster of kids.

"Too hard," a kid on the next machine said without looking over. "Nobody plays it anymore. I'm surprised they don't get rid of it."

"How hard?" Jimmy asked. He twirled the quarter around between his fingers. He loved hard games.

"Ridiculously hard. Don't waste your money. I only ever saw one kid who was good at it, and he doesn't come around anymore." The kid jerked his hand on the joystick and cursed. Then he stomped away. Jimmy realized he'd distracted the kid.

He walked all around the arcade twice. But nothing else was a quarter.

"Probably a total waste," he said.

He dropped the coin into the slot. Then he pushed the start button. The GET READY message scrolled on, then faded. To Jimmy's surprise, the graphics were pretty good for an old machine. And the game was more fun than he'd expected. It was basically a first-person shooter. He was flying a futuristic fighter ship, battling against waves of alien attackers.

The other kid was right—the game was hard. But Jimmy seemed to have a knack for it. He beat the first wave, and then the second. By the time he'd defeated the seventh wave, he hadn't even taken one hit. *Definitely my kind of game*, he thought.

As he cleared wave thirty and waited for the bonus points to add up, he glanced around. The arcade was almost empty. He wondered whether the owner was going to make him leave before his game was finished.

At wave fifty, he heard someone walk up behind him. When he had a chance, he glanced over his shoulder. There was a guy there with a broom.

"Are you closing?" Jimmy asked.

"Yeah, but that's okay. I have to clean up the place and count the change. Keep playing. I understand."

"Thanks."

Jimmy kept playing. His arms started to hurt, but the game was so much fun—and he was so good at it—that he didn't mind.

Wave seventy-five came and went. The game grew harder with each round, but Jimmy got better.

When he cleared wave 127, he was startled to see a GAME OVER message flash on the screen.

"Hey—why did it end?"

The man walked over to him. "That's as hard as it would ever get."

"What do you mean?"

"During the real invasion."

"Huh?" Jimmy had no idea what he was talking about.

"This isn't a game," the man said. "It's a simulator. We need to find kids who have what it takes to defeat an invasion of the Krellex."

If this is real, it's the coolest thing that's ever happened to me, Jimmy thought. He pictured himself leading an army of gamers in a space war against some hideous enemy. But he was still pretty sure the guy was just playing around. "You aren't serious," Jimmy said.

"I sure am. The Krellex armada is on its way. Let me show you." He went behind the counter and pressed a button. A three-dimensional image formed in front of Jimmy, showing a scene from deep space. The man pressed other buttons, and the image zoomed toward a fleet of ships that looked just like the ones Jimmy had blown out of the sky in the game.

"That's them?" he asked.

The man nodded.

"And that's who I'll be blowing out of the sky?" He figured the real thing would be a thousand times better than the game.

"Not exactly," the man said. He flipped a switch, and the image vanished.

"What do you mean?"

"That's who I can't let you blow out of the sky," the man said. "You're far too good. Your reflexes are perfect for battling us." As he walked toward Jimmy, his face seemed to flicker like it was a projection.

For an instant, Jimmy saw the real face of the Krellex. Then the man put his hand on Jimmy's shoulder. Something stung him.

"There are so many of you," the man said as the world around Jimmy started to grow fuzzy. "It's a good thing you are so easy to find. And so easy to defeat. If your brains were as sharp as your reflexes, my people would be in trouble."

THE TASTE OF TERROR

She keeps us in cages. Seven of us. Three boys and three other girls. There were eight of us, but the little boy in the cage next to me screamed himself out this morning. He's gone. I don't know where she took him, but I know we'll never see him again.

She'll find someone else to fill the cage. She has to. There's no end to her hunger. And there's no shortage of us. I was foolish enough to walk into the woods beyond our village in search of mushrooms, even though I'd heard a thousand tales of the dangers that lurked among the ancient oaks. I had no choice. Our family was hungry.

The witch caught me in a snare trap and dragged me to her cottage with the help of a pair of bloodred foxes. I know my father looked for me. He must have. But this place is hidden. I think it is protected by magic. That was a month ago. Maybe longer. I tried to scratch a mark on the wall for each day, but sometimes I forget.

It wouldn't be so bad if she wanted a servant or a companion, though she is hideously ugly to look at. It would be terrible but short if she wanted my flesh. I am not so lucky as to have died quickly. She feeds off our screams.

It was easy for her to draw a scream from me at first. All she had to do was thrust her misshapen face close to mine and cackle. As her acid breath burned my eyes, I screamed so hard, I thought my throat would tear.

I still scream. But something inside me is dying like the last ember in an untended fireplace. I almost don't care what happens to me. That is how weary I am. Terror slowly replaces itself with emptiness. I wonder if I'm ready to be silent. Each time I have that thought, I see my sisters and my youngest brother. One of them could be next. Or my friend Marah from the village. She never watches where she is going.

The witch is evil, but she's also smart. She gives us anything we ask for. The boy in the next cage—he wanted to draw. She gave him charcoal and paper. She left him alone for a whole day. Then she burst in and shredded his drawings.

He shrieked. I could see her quivering with pleasure as she devoured his screams. He lashed out at her with his fists. It did no good. She has spells that keep her from harm. A girl who tried to kick her yesterday ended up with a broken foot. Last month, a boy tried to stab her with his hunting knife. The blade snapped. I doubt it would have made a difference if his strike had plunged true. A witch as evil as she must surely lack a heart.

Our cages are sealed with spells, too. There is no way out. We've whispered to one another our dreams of destroying her, but nobody knows if there is any way to harm her. Surely, there must be. I've heard that witches perish in water. I've also heard they perish in fire. It doesn't matter. I have neither.

Twice this week, she's asked me what I desire. I guess she

knows I'm running dry of screams and she hopes to milk a few more meals from my terror and despair. I didn't want another reason to scream, but as miserable as my life was, I realized I wasn't ready for it to end. I needed to ask for something. I looked across the room at the youngest boy, who was huddled in a corner, shivering. Maybe I could do something for him. As I thought of that, I realized that I might be able to do something for all of them.

"A scarf," I said. "My mother was teaching me to knit. I never finished the scarf I was making. . . ." I stopped. It was too much to hope for.

"How special," she whispered.

That evening, after she feasted on the screams of one of the older girls, she dropped a small cloth sack into my cage.

I waited until she left. My fingers shook as I reached inside. Yarn. Two skeins. And wooden knitting needles.

Perhaps it was folly to make anything. She'd just take it from me and destroy it. I knew that. We all knew that. Whatever she gave us, it was all for one purpose. But my own purpose gave me strength.

I started to knit. The memory came back. Sitting by the fire in our hut. Mother and my sisters knitting or sewing. Father sharpening his tools while my brothers crafted arrows and boasted of their hunting skills.

I knitted all night. I wanted to finish the scarf before it was ripped from my hands. I was just casting off the last stitch when the witch's shadow fell across me.

"How lovely." Her mouth twitched, as if the word *lovely* hurt her tongue.

She opened the cage and bent toward me. I let the scarf drop from the needles. She bent farther.

I screamed. Not out of fear, but for courage and strength. Before she could move, I plunged the needles into her ears, hoping that this might be her one weakness. If the screams could enter her body that way, maybe other things could, too. If I was wrong, I'd know as soon as the needles snapped.

I wasn't wrong. The needles sank in, all the way to where I had them clutched in my fists.

She screamed, staggered away from me, and grabbed the needles. She pulled hard, yanking them from her ears.

She threw the needles to the floor, then grabbed me by the throat. Around me, I could see the cage doors swing open. I'd hurt her enough to weaken her spells.

But I'd done something more important than that. "You're deaf!" I shouted as she squeezed.

"Deaf!" the others shouted.

She didn't seem to hear them. Her fingers crushed my throat. My brain screamed for air. I felt myself grow weak and dizzy. It didn't matter. Now that she could no longer hear our screams, the witch would starve to death. I'd defeated her. My brothers and sisters would be safe. My friend Marah could wander the woods without danger of snare traps.

The others raced into my cage and pried the witch's hands from my throat. She struggled, and tossed some of them aside like dolls, but she seemed to grow weaker with each moment. One of the larger boys looped the scarf around the witch's neck and tied it to the bars. That gave us a chance to escape.

We fled from the cottage into the forest. I blinked against the sunlight, unable to believe I was free. In the trees, a bird sang. The sound was sweet in my ears. It didn't feed my body, but it fed my spirit, filling some of the emptiness that had been left behind by my screams.

THE CAT ALMOST
GETS A BATH

The Sanderson family was allergic to cats. Dad Sanderson was a little bit allergic. Mom Sanderson was very allergic. The kids, Albert and Grace Sanderson, were fairly allergic.

For some reason, the Sanderson family owned a cat. When people asked why they would own something they were allergic to, the best answer they could come up with was, "We don't know."

The Sandersons went through boxes of tissues the way most families went through quarts of milk. At any particular time, there was a good chance that some Sanderson was sneezing, sniffling, or dripping.

One morning, when Dad Sanderson was reading the magazine that came with the Sunday paper, he jumped up and said, "By golly, here's the answer to our problems!" He paused to glance over at Pussums Sanderson, the orange tabby who caused the family to sneeze and sniffle and drip so much.

"What is it, dear?" Mom Sanderson asked.

"It says here that a cat doesn't cause allergies if you give it a bath once a week."

"Give the cat a bath?" Grace asked.

"That's what it said," Dad told her. "And that's exactly what we'll do."

Pussums, with that amazing radar that cats possess, had already snuck from the room. It took a half hour for the rest of the Sandersons to find her and carry her to the bathroom.

"There, there, Pussums," Mom Sanderson said as she started to lower the cat into a sink that was filled with lukewarm water.

Pussums scratched Mom Sanderson about five hundred times in five hundred places.

"Here, dear, let me try," Dad Sanderson said, reaching for the cat.

Mom Sanderson gladly handed Pussums over.

Dad Sanderson quickly received scratches in about seven hundred places.

"Let us try," Albert and Grace said as they reached for Pussums.

Between them, they probably got about thirteen hundred scratches. Pussums leaped from their arms and escaped— high, dry, and unbathed.

Mom Sanderson got out the Band-Aids. Dad Sanderson got out the antiseptic ointment. Mom and Dad and Albert and Grace all started swelling and puffing up like birthday balloons. They might have been allergic to the cat, but they were *really* allergic to cat scratches.

"You know," Dad Sanderson said as he finished unwrapping Band-Aid number two thousand, "I really don't mind suffering through a bit of the sniffles now and then."

"Yes," Mom Sanderson agreed, "there are certainly worse things than a little bitty allergy."

"We can live with it," Grace and Albert said.

Off in a corner of the living room, Pussums sneezed. She was a little allergic, too, but as long as the humans took a bath every day, it wasn't a big problem. As far as Pussums was concerned, she could live with it.

YESTERDAY TOMORROW

It started last week. Though I guess it would make more sense to say it started next week—not that I've been able to make total sense out of this. Anyhow, on Sunday night, Mom made me go to bed early because there was school the next day. I was pretty angry, because I was right near the end of this cool movie. I tried to talk Mom into letting me stay up, but she wouldn't listen.

When I got to my room, I smacked my clock. It went flying off my dresser and hit the wall so hard, the case cracked. Good. It was a stupid clock, anyhow. It showed the time, but it also had the day of the week and the month and all that stuff, like I didn't already know it was Sunday night, May 3.

When I woke, I wondered why I wasn't still half asleep, like I usually was on a Monday. It was bright outside. Definitely past the time I got up for school.

I rushed downstairs. Mom and Dad were at the kitchen table, eating bagels.

"Hi, sleepyhead," Mom said.

"Grab a bagel," Dad said.

Dad always goes out for bagels on Saturday. But it wasn't Saturday—it was Monday.

But if it was Monday, why wasn't Mom frantically packing a lunch and yelling at me to get ready for the bus?

I sat at the table, feeling like I'd been thumped on the head. As the day passed, I discovered it really was Saturday. That's what the newspaper said. And that's what kind of shows were on TV—Saturday cartoons. I'd already watched them this weekend, but I didn't mind seeing them again. That's one of the good things about cartoons—you can watch them over and over.

Even my cracked clock was still working, because it also showed that it was Saturday. The weird thing was that as the day passed, I could see the dial with the days of the week slowly turning, and it looked like it was going backwards.

The next morning, I woke up to find it was Friday. The only bad thing about that was I had to go to school. Thursday followed Friday. By the time Wednesday came, the pattern was obvious. I was waking up a day earlier each morning. The day itself ran forward. I got up in the morning and went to bed at night. But I was moving backwards through the week. And the month.

That should have creeped me out. And it did for a little bit—until I sprained my ankle in gym class. It hurt like crazy. But not for long. I went to bed in pain, and I woke up fine in the morning.

That's when I realized that anything I did to myself wouldn't last. If I broke a bone, it would only hurt for the rest of that day. Even if I got hurt so bad that I passed out, I'd wake up just fine in the morning.

If I got in a fight, the kid I hit wouldn't be angry with me the next day. For him, the fight had never happened. I could beat someone up after school, and never worry about the consequences. If I didn't do my homework, nobody would ever know. If I ate three bowls of ice cream, I didn't have to worry about the calories. Whatever I did, there would be no long-term consequences. No permanent record. No lasting breaks or scars.

The only thing that remained broken was the clock. The crack in the case was always there. The wheels always turned the wrong way. I tried changing the date so I could stay in the weekend, but the control was jammed. I didn't waste much energy worrying about the clock. I had other things on my mind.

I went after the ice cream big-time. A half gallon a day. The best part was that Mom never noticed, because each morning happened before the day I ate the ice cream. Even when I got caught with an empty carton and a spoon, and yelled at for being a pig, there wasn't any real punishment. Each new morning erased everything I'd done the day before. My parents had no more idea I'd done something wrong than our goldfish did.

I learned to skateboard. Even bad breaks were bearable as long as I knew they'd be gone the next morning. There was only one problem—I was getting younger. That was fine for now, since I got smarter and smarter than all the kids in my class. Tests were no trouble when all they asked about was easy stuff. I never even had to study anymore. But I didn't want to go so far back that I ended up in kindergarten.

A year passed. And then another. When I found I couldn't reach the top shelf in my closet, I knew I had to swing time back around so it moved in the right direction.

I was afraid to break the clock, since that could stop it from running, and I didn't want to get frozen in time. Or maybe it would just stop the days from changing. But I didn't want to get stuck that way, either, especially now that I was little. I wanted time to move ahead. I figured the best thing was to try to fix it.

I'd miss the ice cream and the thrill of taking ridiculous risks, but I really didn't want to end up in kindergarten, or in a crib. So, right before I went to bed, I unplugged the clock, opened it, and looked inside. There was a bent lever, and one of the gears had fallen off. I straightened the lever, replaced the gear, and put the case together. Then, I plugged the clock back in. As soon as I did, the display spun forward so fast, the dates blurred.

I felt as if I was spinning along with the display. I got so dizzy, I dropped down on my bed. The whole room seemed to be spinning now. The pressure grew so intense, I realized I was going to pass out. As my consciousness slipped away, I wondered whether I really wanted to move forward. I reached for the plug, but I never made it.

I woke up in pain. I was hit with such an unbelievable tidal wave of agony that I almost passed out. Everything ached. Especially my legs. I wanted to look at them, but something was in my way. I tried to raise my head. I could barely move it.

The thing that blocked my view rose and fell like a living creature. At first, I thought I'd been pinned to the bed by some hideous formless monster. Then I realized the thing moved when I breathed. When I gasped, a ripple shot through it.

Oh, no. The beast was my stomach. It was gigantic—so large, it blocked my view and pinned me on my back. I raised an arm. Rolls of fat hung from it. It was too heavy to hold up for more than a second. I dropped my arm back to the bed as sharp pains burned through my nerves and bones.

I turned my head to the side. The clock was there, set back to the very day and date when I'd broken it. I'd returned to the present like a stretched rubber band, along with all the broken bones and smashed joints I'd picked up in my journey through the past. Along with scrapes and cuts. Along with all the ice cream, candy, pizza, and other food I'd gorged on. Along with every single bad thing I'd done to my body. Even my teeth ached. As I pushed my tongue against them, one fell out. The rest felt loose.

I swatted at the clock, but it was beyond my reach. All I could do was look at it as each agonizing minute ticked by. Today was a nightmare. I knew tomorrow wouldn't be any better. All I had for comfort was memories of yesterday, and those were quickly fading.

TAKE A WHACK AT THIS

The phone connection was pretty bad. That wasn't surprising, since Stan's dad was calling from the Brazilian rain forest. Even so, it was good enough for Stan to hear him say, "I can't be home in time for your birthday. But I'm sending you a surprise."

"Dad's sending me a surprise for my birthday," Stan said after he'd hung up. He was sad that his dad wouldn't be there, but he was used to it. His dad traveled all over the world, studying plants, insects, and animals.

"That's great," his mom said. "A surprise present will make the day really special. Maybe we should have a party."

Stan wasn't sure about that. He'd had a couple parties, but they weren't all that much fun. Mostly, the kids sat around, ate potato chips, and stared at one another while they waited for the cake. But maybe his dad would send him something so incredibly cool that a party would actually be fun.

Stan checked the porch each day for a package. Finally, one week before his birthday, he found a large box right outside the door. He tore it open and discovered a giant ball.

But it wasn't the kind of ball you play with. It was covered with red, yellow, and green stripes. There was no note or card—just a slip of paper with the word PIÑATA.

"Cool." Stan knew what a piñata was. They were filled with candy. Kids would wear a blindfold and swing a bat until someone connected hard enough to smash the piñata open and spill the candy.

He took the package up to his room, then told his mom, "I decided I want a party." He didn't mention the piñata. She wasn't big on candy, and he suspected she really wasn't big on blindfolded kids swinging baseball bats.

Stan invited all his friends. And since that was only two kids, he also invited a lot of his other classmates. He couldn't help bragging to everyone that he had a supersecret surprise.

The morning of Stan's birthday, his mom set up a table in the backyard with chips and soda. Stan waited until she went inside. Then he tied a rope around the piñata and hung it over a tree branch.

"Cool, a piñata," Trevor said when he arrived. All the other kids had the same reaction. Stan checked to make sure his mom wasn't coming out, then grabbed the bat and large handkerchief he'd hidden behind the garage. "Who wants to go first?" he said. Not that it mattered. He planned to control the rope so that nobody else could hit the piñata. After all, it was his present. He was the one who should have the fun of whacking it.

His plan worked. Everyone missed. "I guess it's up to me." Stan handed the rope to Trevor, who was so amazingly uncoordinated, he'd never pull the rope at the right time to avoid the piñata's destruction. Then he grabbed the bat, put on the blindfold, and got ready to give the piñata a beating.

Inside, Stan's mom was reading the mail. There was a letter from her husband. He started out with, "I'm sending home some amazing specimens I've collected. There's a large box coming. It contains the egg case of a giant piñata spider. Be careful not to break it. It's perfectly safe as long as it remains intact. But the spiders are incredibly aggressive once they are released."

Stan's mom frowned. She hadn't seen any large package. Just the small one that came that morning with Stan's present. She hadn't told him about it yet. She figured she'd let him open it during the party. That would be fun for all the kids. She thought about asking him whether he'd seen a large box. But he was busy with his friends. She could ask him after the party was over.

It was only slightly later—maybe a minute at the most—when she heard the first screams coming from the backyard. Screams, shrieks, and some minor crashes. She couldn't help smiling. It definitely sounded like the kids were running all over the place. Her son's shouts seemed to be the loudest of all. His squeals of joy made her feel good.

"Those kids are really having a fun time," she said as she settled in her chair and sipped a cup of tea. "I hope the neighbors don't mind a little noise."

KING OF THE HILL

As soon as I heard the high-pitched voices and the clatter of stones in the distance, I tried to lead Duncan away from the slag pile. But I guess Duncan's hearing is just as good as mine. Or maybe even better. Predators have great hearing. Duncan might not be a wolf or a jaguar, but he definitely responded to the sound of potential prey.

"Hey, let's go to the mall," I said as he started to cut through the woods.

"The mall's for losers." He sped up. The voices were clearer now. It sounded like seven or eight of them.

I chased after him. We broke through the trees, and I saw them. Looked like second- or third-graders, climbing over the slag heap of broken shale we called Bare Head Mountain. It wasn't a mountain—just a hill covered with loose stone. It had three boulders at the top. The one in the middle looked sort of like part of a head. The kids were pushing, laughing, rolling, and having a great time, screaming, "I'm king of the hill," as they fought to stay on the top.

"Wrong." Duncan jabbed his thumb at his chest. "I'm

king of the hill. They just don't know it yet. But they're gonna learn."

"Come on, this isn't any fun," I said.

"It will be." He jogged ahead.

I stood for a moment, wondering whether to leave. Duncan liked to play rough. And he didn't seem to care who he played with. He was just as happy tossing around a couple third-graders as he was tackling a middle school kid. There was no way I could stop him. He'd kick my butt and enjoy every second, even though I was supposed to be his best friend.

Duncan was already at the bottom of the hill. He reached out and grabbed a kid who was just scrambling up. He actually lifted the kid off his feet before he flung him backwards.

The kid landed facedown. He got up on his hands and knees, then fell again. The rest of the kids didn't seem to notice. I guess they were still too busy trying to be king of the hill.

I walked over to the fallen kid. He turned his tear-streaked face toward me, then gasped like I was some sort of movie monster.

"You okay?" I asked.

He nodded and made wet, gulping sounds.

"You might want to take off."

He got up and tottered toward the woods. Another kid landed at the bottom of the hill. He sat up, then clutched his shoulder.

Duncan had gotten about halfway to his goal, and so far, he'd taken out four kids. The kid at the top had the advantage of being able to see what was happening. He turned and scrambled down the other side of the heap. The two remaining little kids kept tugging at each other, trying to become the new king. They didn't have a clue that the game was about to change.

Duncan grabbed them by their shoulders and flung his arms out, tossing the kids aside. They came to a rest at the bottom of the hill, slumped like rag dolls.

I made sure neither of them had broken anything, then watched as they fled into the woods.

"I'm king of the hill," Duncan said.

"Yup."

"Try to knock me down."

"No thanks."

"Come on. It's no fun by myself."

"I'm going home." I turned away.

"No."

The word sent a chill through me. The way he said it, I felt like a dog being yelled at. I sighed and started to climb the hill. I figured I'd give it a good effort, try to avoid getting injured when he pushed me down, and then pretend I was too hurt to play anymore.

Halfway to the top, I paused.

"Scared?" Duncan asked.

I didn't answer. I was watching the boulder to his left. It had moved. Not like it was rolling. But—and I know this sounds crazy—like it was expanding.

"Come on, wuss! Come knock me off."

I took another step. The boulder expanded a bit more.

"Why don't you come down. It's dangerous up there."

"Why don't you knock me down?" He tilted his head back and spat in the air. I dodged as the loogie arced down toward me.

The boulder kept expanding. No. It wasn't expanding. That wasn't the right word. It was unfolding.

Duncan stooped, grabbed a rock, and lobbed it in my direction. I guess he was out of spit.

The boulder continued to unfold, like a fist unclenching. The rock Duncan threw at me cracked against the slag a yard to my left.

The fist was fully unclenched now. The boulder on the other side of Duncan also started to open.

"Look!" I shouted, pointing to the stone hands on either side of him.

"Nice try." He grabbed another rock.

The hands jutted to the side. Loose rocks and slag slid down the hill as arms extended.

He rose. He. It. Whatever you call a slag hill with arms and legs and a crude head. He rose to his feet. I tumbled from mine and rolled to the ground.

I looked up. Duncan was atop the rock head, screaming, "King of the hill! King of the hill!"

One rock hand reached up, curled a forefinger, and flicked Duncan off. He sailed over my head and landed somewhere in the woods.

In the face, stone lips moved—slowly, as if it had been centuries since they last parted. The voice, a low rumble like the groan of a rock slide, spoke. "The hill is king of itself."

I stood there, frozen, as he folded back down. Then I turned and ran into the woods, wondering whether Duncan could have survived.

I found him a hundred yards away, lying on his stomach across a fallen tree. His shirt had been shredded by the branches that broke his fall. He had the groggy eyes of a boxer who'd just lost fifteen straight rounds. His leg was bent the wrong way. His face was cut and bleeding. The injuries were bad, but not fatal.

The little kids had found him, too. They were taking turns climbing up on his back and shouting, "I'm king of the bully."

I thought about chasing them off, but it looked like they were having a lot of fun, and they didn't seem to be hurting him all that much.

"The hill is king of itself," I told Duncan. I figured it was worth sharing the message.

"What?" He seemed puzzled. Maybe he was too stunned from his fall to understand. Or maybe he was the sort of kid who could never believe anything was better or stronger than he was. Not even after he'd been turned into a piece of living playground equipment. It didn't matter. I understood the message.

I headed off to get help. Duncan would need a lot of patching up. He'd need plenty of medical attention. And he'd need to find someone else to hang out with.

BOOK BANNING

Morley Blezner slunk into the school library, paused to glare at Ms. Dawner, the librarian, and Mr. Lawrence, the library assistant, and then stomped over to the shelves. He'd rather be almost anywhere else. Books were stupid. The library was stupid. But he had to pick a book for a report. And he didn't have any at home. So he had no choice.

Ms. Dawner walked over to him, all smiley and cheerful. "Can I help you find something?"

"No." Morley turned away from her. He could find his own book. He was sure she'd give him something really bad. Something thick and important. He wanted to get away from her before she tried to offer more help. He walked between two rows of shelves, so he'd be out of sight, and pulled a thin book out at random.

There was a spaceship on the cover. "Cool," he said. He opened the book and saw it was filled with pictures from science fiction movies. He spotted a page with a scene from his favorite movie. "Awesome!"

He thought about taking the book out. But he wasn't

interested in the rest of the pictures. He checked over his shoulder. Nobody could see him. Slowly, carefully, so it wouldn't make any sound, he ripped the page from the book. Then he slid the book back on the shelf.

As he turned away, something slammed against the back of his head.

"Hey!" Morley spun around, ready to throw a punch. But nobody had hit him. He looked at the floor. The book was there, like it had flown off the shelf. Another book, a lot thicker than the first, shot at him from a lower shelf, bouncing off his chest.

"Ow!" Morley staggered back.

More books flew at him from both sides. He turned and ran, fleeing through a hail of books.

The books drove him out of the aisle and across the library. He raced toward the door. Before he got there, he had to pass the reference section. He almost didn't make it out alive. A couple encyclopedia volumes, a world atlas, and a whopping unabridged dictionary did major damage.

Finally, Morley escaped through the double doors. Crying, gasping, bloody and bruised, he limped down the hall toward his class.

"Well, he's gone," Mr. Lawrence said as the doors hissed shut behind Morley.

"You know," Ms. Dawner said, "I'm still not sure book banning is a good idea."

"It'll do until something better comes along," Mr. Lawrence said. "I just wish the process didn't make such a mess." He sighed, and started putting the books back on the shelves.

BRACES

Until she stepped into Dr. Kublanko's waiting room, Shelly felt pretty good about getting braces. Half the popular kids in school wore them, and Shelly did have to admit that her overbite made her look more than a little bit like a bunny. She got tons of advice from her friends once she spread the news.

"Chew lots of gum now," Sarah told her, "because you won't be chewing any once they put the braces on."

"Plan on eating spaghetti for the first few days," Lorie warned her. "You won't feel like chewing."

Now, she was just minutes away from her first session in the chair. It was only an exam, but it brought her that much closer to the moment when it all became real. The waiting room was so dim and gloomy, Shelly paused right inside the doorway.

"Don't worry," her mother said. "They'll be off again before you know it."

Shelly nodded and sat on a couch that was wedged against one wall. A younger girl was slumped in a chair across the room. When she looked up, Shelly smiled.

The girl's head drooped back down.

"He's very reasonable," Shelly's mother said, whispering the last word. Shelly knew that *reasonable* was her mother's way of saying *cheap*.

That could definitely describe the waiting room. The place certainly didn't resemble any other office she'd been in. It smelled more like an antique shop than a dentist's office. The furniture was old and worn. There weren't any magazines. There was no music or radio. There wasn't even a receptionist.

Dr. Kublanko popped into the waiting room and said, "Shelly?" He looked almost too young to be a dentist.

"That's me," Shelly said. She followed him as he bounced down a short dark hall to a room with a dentist's chair. When she looked at the chair, a pang rippled through her stomach. For an instant, she thought of turning and fleeing. What was so terrible about a few crooked teeth?

"Hop right up," Dr. Kublanko said.

Shelly got in the chair.

"Let's have a look," he said.

Shelly opened her mouth. Dr. Kublanko examined her for a moment, then said, "Well, let's get started."

"What?"

"The braces," Dr. Kublanko said.

"But, don't you have to do some X-rays? Isn't this just an exam?"

"Oh, you need braces. And there's no point in waiting. So let's get them on."

Dr. Kublanko went to work. It took a lot less time than Shelly expected. The doctor just slipped something over all her teeth. One minute, she was sitting there with her mouth open; a moment later, she was aware of this strange *thing* against her lips.

"It feels funny," Shelly tried to say. But it came out "Ih eel zunny."

"You'll get used to it," Dr. Kublanko said. "I'll see you again in exactly one week."

Shelly slid out of the chair. It was odd—she'd assumed the strange metal in her mouth would feel cold, but it was very warm.

She probed the braces with her tongue. They felt weird.

"That wasn't so bad, was it?" her mom asked when Shelly returned to the waiting room.

"Gesh not," Shelly said, which was as close to *guess not* as she could come at the moment. She wondered when it would start to hurt. Her friends told her that her teeth might ache for a day or two.

That evening, she still felt fine. There was no ache, no discomfort at all other than the strangeness in her mouth. She was almost completely used to her braces by the time she went to sleep. She halfway woke up once in the middle of the night, and had the strangest feeling that she didn't have her braces on. *I must be getting used to them,* she thought as she fell back to sleep.

In the morning, her mouth felt fine. No pain, no discomfort. She wondered how the braces could work if she didn't feel anything. At her next appointment, she asked Dr. Kublanko about that.

"Oh, these are the latest design," he said as he examined her. "Everything is going perfectly." He took a thin hose with a nozzle at the end and put it inside her mouth.

"What are you doing?" Shelly asked, speaking around the nozzle.

"Oh, just cleaning things a bit. Hmmmm. From the way these look, I'm guessing you breathe through your nose. Try to breathe through your mouth. The braces work best when they get lots of air."

That didn't make sense. Shelly was going to say something, but she suddenly felt very tired. She blinked. Had she dozed? She looked up at the doctor. "There," he was saying. "All set until next week."

"Uh, okay." Shelly still felt strange. Her eyes wandered round the small room, settling for a moment on a diploma hanging above the sink. Shelly looked at the date. Dr. Kublanko had gotten his degree more than forty years ago. That didn't make sense. He couldn't possibly be that old.

"Relax," the dentist told her. "Everything is progressing just the way it's supposed to. Now get along home."

On the way out, Shelly saw a girl in the waiting room. The girl smiled at her and said, "I'm just here to see if I need braces."

Don't go in there. Shelly almost spoke, but she was too tired to find the right words. It wasn't worth the effort. She dropped her head and turned away.

Shelly woke again in the middle of the night. Something glinted on the windowsill, right up against the screen. Shelly started to get up, but the room danced in circles and slid from under her. As she fell back to sleep, she felt something slipping onto her teeth.

"I want to get my braces off," she told her mom the next morning.

"But that's ridiculous, dear," her mom said. "You need to

wear them for at least two years. Otherwise, they won't do any good. What's wrong? Are the other girls teasing you?"

Shelly shook her head. She saw there was no use trying to explain it to her mom. But the dentist was another matter. She'd talk to him at her next appointment.

"And how are you?" he asked Shelly as he tilted her chair.

"There's something wrong with my braces," she said.

"Oh, really? Well, it's easy to adjust these things." He reached onto his tray and took up a small pliers. "What exactly is the problem?"

They leave my mouth and crawl around the room at night. That's what Shelly wanted to say. But, suddenly, she was afraid to admit that she knew this. Shelly looked at his face—it was so young, except for his eyes. She turned away, scared to stare into those eyes. "Uh, they feel a bit loose," she said.

"Oh, dear. Here, see if this is better." He did something inside her mouth.

Shelly nodded. "Much better," she said when the dentist had removed the tool.

"Good. Now let me do just one more thing." He placed another tool, the one connected to a hose, into her mouth. "Great," he said a moment later. "All done."

Shelly realized she was nearly asleep. She dragged herself from the chair and staggered out of the office. When she got home, she fell right into bed and slept without waking during the night.

The next morning, Shelly looked carefully at her teeth in the mirror. Nothing seemed to have changed. Then she looked at her face. She was tired. There were dark bags under her eyes. Her face seemed older; her hair seemed dry and brittle.

I didn't look like this before, she thought. It had all changed after her first visit with Dr. Kublanko. She touched her cheek. The skin felt more like wax than flesh. She was sure that her youth and energy were being stolen. It had to be the braces. That night, she set her alarm to ring at three thirty in the morning. *It's going to end,* Shelly thought as she lay down in her bed.

The alarm jolted her. She sat up and switched it off.

Her tongue ran across bare teeth. She looked around the room. The braces, like a metal spider, were on the windowsill, sitting in the moonlight. As she caught sight of them, they rushed toward her.

"No!" Shelly shouted.

The braces scurried to the bed and sprang up onto the mattress.

Shelly clamped her hand across her mouth.

Sharp wires dug into her skin as the braces climbed her nightshirt. Wires stabbed at the hand she'd clamped across her mouth.

Shelly grabbed the braces with her other hand and ripped them free. She flung them to the floor. They started to charge back toward her. Shelly rolled to the floor and slammed her fist down on the braces. They flattened, but sprang right back into shape. She kept hitting them. Over and over, she slammed the braces. It took every bit of strength she had. The world wavered. She felt more drained with each strike. Shelly wondered if she was going to pass out.

"*Shelly!* What's going on? Why are you on the floor?"

Shelly opened her eyes, sat up slowly, and looked at her mother standing in the doorway. "My braces," she said.

Her mother switched on the light and knelt next to

Shelly. She put a hand under Shelly's chin and looked at her mouth. "What about them? They seem just fine."

Shelly started to speak. The braces rubbed against her tongue. She looked at the spot on the floor. It was bare.

"You'd better get some sleep, young lady," her mother said. "You have school tomorrow. Oh, and I almost forgot. Dr. Kublanko called. He needs to make another adjustment to your braces. You have an appointment with him tomorrow, right after school." She paused and shook her head. "I honestly don't see how he can give so many appointments and charge so little. But I'm certainly not complaining."

Shelly nodded, unable to speak. Tired and drained of energy, she crawled back to bed. *It must be my imagination,* she thought. *It was a dream or something.*

"It doesn't matter," Shelly whispered. She was too exhausted to care. She felt so tired, and so old. Nothing was important—not the braces on her teeth, not even the cuts and scratches on her hands. Shelly had no idea how those small injuries had gotten there, but they didn't matter, either. The cuts would heal. And in just a few years, she'd have nice, straight teeth. Wouldn't that be wonderful?

TURKEY CALLS

Hey, look at this." Chester handed a copy of his favorite magazine, *Time Wasters*, to his brother Wyatt. He pointed at the picture. "I'm going to make one of those."

"A turkey call?" Wyatt asked. "Why would you want to make something like that?"

"Why not?" Chester said. "Come on, it looks easy. And it will be a great way to waste some time." Chester ran around the house, gathering up the materials that were listed in the instructions.

"Well," he said a half hour later as he stood in front of an impressive pile of turkey call parts, "I guess that's everything we need."

"Not really," Wyatt said. "You got the stuff all wrong. The article said you needed a piece of iron. That's aluminum."

"So? It's still metal," Chester said. "That's close enough. It's not like I'm building a helicopter."

"And the piece of wood is supposed to be six inches wide. That looks bigger. If you don't follow the directions, it's not going to work right."

"I'm not allowed to use the saw when Dad isn't around," Chester said. "Besides, it doesn't really matter."

"But the article said—"

"It doesn't matter. Come on—let's put it together." Chester got to work. Wyatt helped. In another half hour, the turkey call was finished.

Chester tried it out, scraping the metal bar against the piece of slate inside the small box. "Wow—it *does* sound like a turkey."

Wyatt shook his head. "I don't know. Maybe it sounds a little like a turkey. It also sort of sounds like a cat or a monkey, or maybe even some kind of giant rat. Who knows what it'll attract?"

Chester glared at his brother. "Look, if that's what you think, I'll go out and use it by myself."

"No, I want to come," Wyatt said.

"Then stop telling me I did it wrong. I think it sounds exactly like a turkey."

Chester went outside and headed down the street toward the woods at the edge of town. He heard Wyatt behind him. By the time they reached the woods, he wasn't angry anymore. He was excited. Following one of the foot trails, he walked far into the woods.

"This looks like a good spot," Chester said. He held up the turkey call and scratched out some awesome sounds.

Almost immediately, even before Wyatt could say anything else to make fun of Chester, there was a rustling in the bushes. There was a lot of rustling all around them.

"It worked!" Chester used the call again, pressing harder so it was even louder. The more turkeys, the better. That would show Wyatt a thing or two. "It really, really worked."

"Almost," Wyatt said.

"I'm tired of your attitude," Chester said. "Can't you admit it worked just fine?" Then he saw what Wyatt had already noticed. Hundreds of animals burst through the bushes all around him, coming to his call. Animals. Not birds. Small black-and-white animals.

"Skunks," Wyatt said.

"This call stinks," Chester said, throwing it down.

In a moment, the call wasn't the only thing that stank.

REEL

There it is," I said when we reached the old movie theater behind the bowling alley. I hadn't been on this side of town in a long time.

"Man, the place is falling down," Noah said.

"I don't care. It's the only theater showing *Power Drill*." I'd been dying to see that movie ever since I read about it in *Gore and Splatter* magazine. They said it was the scariest, slashiest, wettest horror movie in years. And the bad guy, Fixxula, was unbelievably warped.

"They won't sell us tickets," Noah said. "Let's just go rent a video."

"You go, if you want," I told him. "I'm seeing this movie." I checked the sign again. The place had three movies playing. I'd been hoping at least one would be rated G so I could buy a ticket for it and then sneak into the screen that was showing *Power Drill*. But all three movies were at least PG-13. I was twelve. To make things even worse, I looked young for my age.

"Forget it," Noah said.

"No. We'll sneak in the exit."

"That does it. No way I'm getting in trouble for a stupid movie. I'm outta here." Noah trotted off like he couldn't wait to go rent some boring video.

I didn't care. It's better with a friend—especially during the really messy scenes—but I could enjoy the movie all by myself. I went around to the back and checked out the exit door. It was old, the wood in the frame was rotten, and I could see the bolt didn't close all the way. It hadn't latched the last time someone went out. I tugged at it, and the door opened. Perfect. I slipped inside and looked around. I was in a hallway. That was good.

I spotted the sign for the screen with *Power Drill* and ducked into the room. I didn't want anyone to spot me, so I grabbed a seat in the back row.

My timing was awesome. Just after I sat, the lights dimmed. They showed a couple previews, and then a sign flashed on the screen: THIS FILM IS IN PERCEPTIVISION.

"Cool," I whispered, though I had no idea what that meant.

Another message appeared beneath it: SELECT YOUR AVATAR.

The back of the seat in front of me lit up. I realized there was a small screen in it, like the kind they have on laptop computers. The screen showed a dozen different faces. I figured those were the actors from the movie. It was the usual sort of cast—a brave guy, a scared guy, a funny guy, a pretty girl, and so on. I picked the brave guy, since I figured that would be the most interesting.

A final message came up: ADJUST THE COMFORT LEVEL OF YOUR HEADSET.

Headset? I looked around. Everyone had some sort of red headband, with knobs on the side. I guess they'd been handed out by the ticket taker. There was no way I could get one. I didn't care. The movie would be fine without any gimmicks.

A moment after the movie started, I found out what Perceptivision was. When the brave guy—his name was Rocko—walked out into the rain, my face felt wet. I looked around, trying to figure out how they did that, but I didn't see any hoses or anything.

When the scared guy got his head cut off and Rocko was splashed with the blood, I felt something warm and wet splash my face. It was so realistic, I reached up and touched my cheek, but there was nothing there.

Rocko and Fixxula were chasing each other all over this huge abandoned hardware store. When Rocko tried to punch Fixxula and hit the wall instead, my fist hurt. But not a lot. This was so cool. Noah had really missed out.

Then Fixxula almost caught Rocko. He cut him in the shoulder with a hedge clippers.

"Ow!" My shoulder stung. But it wasn't all that bad. Besides—Rocko was obviously the hero. He might get hurt, but he'd survive. I noticed that people were playing with the dials on their headsets. I guess they could control how much pain they felt. I glanced back toward the entrance, wondering whether it was too late to get myself a headset. But I knew they'd never give me one. It didn't matter. I could handle this.

The next time Rocko was surprised by Fixxula, he got stabbed in the leg with a screwdriver. That hurt a bit more. I started to think about leaving. But I really wanted to see the rest of the movie. I could always leave if it got too painful.

Two more of Rocko's friends got killed by Fixxula. Man—Noah was missing an awesome movie. I couldn't wait to tell him what a loser he was. I checked my watch. The movie was about half over. The action should get even more extreme pretty soon. As I looked back up at the screen, Fixxula jumped Rocko from behind and hit him hard in the head with a toolbox.

My own head jolted. I got dizzy for a second.

"Okay—that's enough." I'd had it. I wasn't going to sit there and let myself get hurt any more—especially not when the bad guy had a whole storeful of power tools, and I didn't have a helmet with a control knob.

I tried to stand. Something held me to my seat. I tried harder. No luck. I couldn't even move my arms. I looked down, but didn't see anything. I looked back up at the screen. Fixxula had tied Rocko to a chair. I could feel the pressure of ropes around my arms and chest.

Fixxula grabbed a nail gun from his table. "This is going to hurt a lot," he said.

I screamed for help. Nobody in the theater turned toward me. They were all screaming, too. Though nowhere near as loudly.

BAD LUCK

I was hanging out in front of the corner store after school, drinking a Coke and killing a bag of garlic pretzels, when the kid came strutting down the street. He had that walk— you know, the walk that says, *I'm cool. Don't mess with me.* When I see someone flashing that attitude, I can't help thinking of ways to prove to him that he's wrong.

"Hey," I said as he passed in front of me. "Who are you?" I didn't recognize him. He wasn't from Madison High, and I didn't think he went to St. Pat's or Winslow Academy, either. He probably came from over in Sunnington.

The kid spun toward me so quickly, I figured I'd startled him. "You noticed me?"

"Hard not to," I told him. My eyes scanned him from top to bottom, then back up. He was wearing cheap sneakers, jeans, a white T-shirt, and a Red Sox jacket. He had on a cap, brim forward, with the letters BL stitched on the front. Beneath the cap was the kind of face ten-year-old girls like to cut out of magazines and grandmothers like to pinch.

And on his face was the kind of smirk kids like me like to erase. "Who are you?" I asked again.

"I'm bad luck," he said.

I laughed. The kid didn't lack guts. I had at least five inches on him, and thirty pounds. I figured I could flick him across the street if I wanted—not that I was in the mood. But I couldn't let the kid's words go unanswered. "You don't look so tough," I told him, getting ready to dodge if he took a swing at me.

He shook his head. "I didn't say I was tough. And I didn't say I was bad luck for you. Though I could be. I said I was *Bad Luck*."

I could hear the capital letters when he spoke, but I still didn't get it. "You're Bad Luck?"

"Yeah." He glanced over his shoulder, then pointed to a car that was coming down Bradshaw Street. "Observe." He snapped his fingers.

Paboom!

The right front tire blew, just like that. The car skidded to a halt, and the driver hopped out. He looked at the tire. Then he kicked the flat and started swearing.

"Bad Luck," the kid said, grinning at me with a smug look like he'd just performed a magic trick.

Before I could say anything, he pointed across the street toward some first-graders walking home from school. "Let me demonstrate." He clapped his hands. The kid in front tripped on the sidewalk and went down hard on his left knee. He started crying. The others laughed and walked ahead.

"You did that?" I asked, remembering when the same thing had happened to me back in second grade.

"Sure did."

I chewed on the information for a moment. "So what you're saying is when a kid catches a baseball in the face, or loses his homework, or gets snagged in the thumb by his own fishhook, you're to blame?"

He made a small bow, then straightened up, still wearing that smug expression. "I can't take credit for every single bit of bad luck on the planet, but I do get around."

"That stinks," I said, stepping away from the wall. I'd had my share of bad luck, but I'd never expected to find myself face-to-face with someone who was responsible for most of it. I thought about a June day two years ago when I'd broken my leg right before summer vacation. Compound fracture. I'd spent half the summer in a cast. "That really stinks."

"Careful," he said. "It's bad luck to pick a fight with Bad Luck."

I curled my fingers into a fist. It would feel so good to flatten him. But he was right. This guy could sink a ship or strike a house with lightning. I'd have to be crazy to mess with him. "I'm not a fool," I told him.

"I didn't think so. Well, it's been charming chatting, but I must be going." He started to walk on past me.

"Hey," I said. "I have to know one thing."

"What?" he asked, turning back toward me.

"Why?"

"No reason," he said.

"There has to be a reason," I told him. "There's a reason the sky is blue. There's a reason leopards have spots. There has to be a reason for bad luck."

I think he was about to answer when he glanced back down the street at a man walking a dog. He got a glint in his eyes as he pointed his finger at the man.

Snap.

The leash broke with a twang and the dog went running. The guy chased after him.

"Sorry, couldn't resist," Bad Luck said. "But, as I was going to tell you, how should I know why I'm here? I just do what I do. And I do it very well. But I can't explain it. I mean, is there any reason *you're* here?"

"Not till now," I said. Before I could talk myself out of it, I closed the distance between us and hit him as hard as I could. I slugged him square in the jaw, and he dropped like a sack full of rocks.

I stared down at him. Now what?

There was no way I could leave him there. He'd find me when he woke up. I didn't want to become Bad Luck's pet project. I lifted him up, threw him over my shoulder, and headed home.

I guess other people couldn't see him, because nobody asked me what I was doing carrying a body down the street. Good thing he wasn't too heavy.

I put him in the room over the garage where my folks store all the old furniture. I tied his hands behind his back. From what I'd seen, he seemed to need them to make stuff happen.

Yeah, it was crazy for me to hit him, but I'd had my share of bad luck, and I figured that, if nothing else, I'd be doing everyone a favor. Naturally, as soon as I finished tying him up, I started to have doubts about the whole thing. He couldn't really be Bad Luck.

But after a day, he hadn't asked for food or begged to use the bathroom. After two days, he hadn't even asked for a drink of water. As far as I could tell from my frequent trips to the garage, he never slept. And every time he looked at me, that stupid smirk twitched across his lips.

A week passed. Then another. "I haven't noticed much of a change," I told him one evening. I'd fallen into the habit of sitting with him, talking. "The world is pretty much the same." Somehow, I'd expected to make a difference.

"I'm not responsible for all the world's problems. Don't forget Stupidity. He's pretty busy. And all the others: Coincidence, Tragedy, Glitch, all those guys. Hey, you should meet Poetic Justice. Talk about a guy who's full of himself."

I thought about those forces running loose in the world, causing problems for a reason nobody knew. Big troubles and small misfortunes. Nothing I did would make a difference.

"Are you the sort who holds a grudge?" I asked.

He shook his head. "We're cool. But don't expect any favors, either."

"Fair enough." As I untied him, I couldn't help laughing.

"What's so funny?" he asked.

"Don't you get it?" I tossed the ropes into the corner of the room. It felt good to laugh.

"Get what?" He stood up from the chair, but he didn't stretch or act stiff, even though he'd been sitting in one position for a couple weeks.

"Think about it," I told him.

He grinned and shrugged. "Not a clue."

"Well, was it *Good Luck* that you ran into someone who could see you and knock you out?"

He stared at me for a while. Finally he admitted the same thing I'd already realized. "I guess it was sort of bad luck. . . ." For once, his smirk faded completely.

"How about that?" I opened the door. When I'd first met

Bad Luck, I'd been furious at the idea of this force, this *thing,* that could cast misfortune about him like a child flinging a handful of gravel on a playground. When he'd told me he didn't even know the reason he was doing it, that had been too much.

He went out and headed down the steps that led to the driveway. Halfway there, he stumbled.

Bad luck.

Even though I was pretty sure he didn't feel any pain, I winced as I watched him tumble to a landing on the hard asphalt.

For a moment, he didn't move. Finally, still lying there on his stomach, he pointed across the street to Mr. Jurgin's house. A tree branch fell from the large maple in the front yard, crunching the roof of Mr. Jurgin's new Porsche. I guess Bad Luck needed to make sure he could still function. He staggered to his feet. He didn't look back as he walked away.

"See you," I said.

He sort of waved over his shoulder. I knew I'd be seeing him again. I'd be seeing him all my life. We all would. There was no escape from Bad Luck. That didn't seem fair. But at least I knew we weren't alone. Bad Luck, and all his buddies out there, had a force to deal with also.

They had their own Bad Luck. I guess they had all the other misfortunes, too. Somehow, that made it all seem just a little bit more fair.

RATTLED NERVES

Jermaine presented a perfectly good argument for why he should be allowed to stay home from school and play video games. "We're just going to be walking in the stupid woods all day, and learning about stupid animals, stupid birds, and stupid plants."

"It's educational," his mom said. "You'll get to be face-to-face with nature."

"I'll get ticks or something," Jermaine said. "You want me to get ticks?"

"You'll be fine." His mom handed him his lunch. "Get going."

So Jermaine found himself on the bus, along with all his classmates, heading for the William Stintz Wildlife Sanctuary.

"This is stupid," he told Barney Emmerson, who had the aisle side of their bus seat.

"Come on, it will be great," Barney said.

"Maybe for nerds," Jermaine said.

An hour later, the bus rolled through the gate of the

wildlife sanctuary, drove past several buildings, and pulled up to the curb next to a large wooden cabin. According to the sign, it was the REPTILE EDUCATION CENTER.

"I didn't think reptiles needed an education," Barney said. He laughed at his own joke.

"That does it," Jermaine muttered. He'd been afraid they'd end up someplace with crawly things. It just wasn't natural for something to slither around without legs. He could see a display of stuffed and mounted snakes through the large window near the front entrance of the cabin. A sign above the display promised: MEET OUR NATIVE WILDLIFE.

"Not me." Jermaine hopped off the bus with the rest of the class, strolled past Ms. Dwetch as she counted heads, went into the building, then dashed out a side door marked NO EXIT before he had to actually look at a snake close up.

He glanced over his shoulder as he moved away from the building, to make sure nobody noticed his escape. That was a mistake. The side door was only a step and a half away from the top of a steep slope. In the middle of his second step, Jermaine lost his footing and stumbled.

"Gah!" he screamed repeatedly as he plummeted toward the bottom of the hill. It was at least a twelve-gah tumble, not that Jermaine counted. He was too busy bouncing off rocks.

Luckily, the thornbushes he rolled over on his way down cushioned his fall just enough so he didn't snap any bones. But by the time he'd skidded to a stop, his left arm wasn't feeling too good, his right knee throbbed like it had been smacked with a golf club, and his face felt like it had been used as a scratching post by at least a dozen cats.

Still on his back, Jermaine looked up the way he'd come. The hill was too steep to climb. He didn't want to risk taking another tumble. But there was a narrow path right in front of him that led around the hill.

He got up, brushed bits of gravel and leaves from his hands, and started to hobble down the path, figuring he'd eventually find an easy way to get back up to the bus. The slope on the other side of the path wasn't so steep, but it was covered with thornbushes all the way up.

"Stupid wildlife . . . ," he muttered. He kept muttering and groaning, which is why he didn't notice anything unusual at first.

When the sound finally caught his attention, he froze in his tracks. At that point, he realized he'd been hearing it for a while. Hearing it, but not really listening.

Until now. Now, it had his full attention.

No way . . .

He listened with both ears. He even tried to listen with his eyes, nose, and skin. Above the sudden thudding of his pulse in his temples, he heard it again.

Shika-shika-shika-sshhhhh.

The rattle came from somewhere behind him.

"Snake," Jermaine whispered. The word, barely spoken, had the power to jack his pulse even higher. He scanned the ground, but didn't spot anything.

The rattle got louder and faster. Jermaine sprinted for the hill on his left. Thornbushes snagged at his legs, but he pushed his way through. A couple feet up the hill, when he stopped to catch his breath, he heard the rattle again. It was closer.

Jermaine forced his way deeper. The bushes grew denser. He pushed the branches away from his face, trying to make a path where no path seemed possible.

"Jermaine . . . ?"

He heard his name shouted in the distance. They were looking for him. They must have spread out through the parking lot, he realized, to check the other buildings.

"Here!" he shouted. "Down here!"

"Where?"

Jermaine recognized Barney's voice. "Up the hill on the other side." He tried to turn around, but he was too tangled to move. A thousand thorns snagged his clothes.

"Why are you up there?" Barney called.

"A rattlesnake was chasing me," Jermaine said. Maybe the other kids would scare off the snake. Or maybe the people who ran the place would catch it. Better yet—maybe they'd kill it.

Barney laughed. "Good one."

"It's not funny!" Jermaine screamed.

"Sure it is. Rattlesnake? Right. There aren't any rattlesnakes around here," Barney said. "We just learned that inside."

"I don't care. Get me out of here."

"I'll tell Ms. Dwetch I found you," Barney said. "Don't worry. I won't mention the snake. No point having everyone laugh at you."

"Wait! Don't go!"

There was no answer. Jermaine listened to the sound of Barney running off. Then he listened to the rattle. It was closer now. But it was more than just close. It was all around him, coming from every bush.

"Help!" Jermaine pictured dozens of snakes slithering toward him, crawling up inside his pants legs and down the back of his shirt, sinking their fangs into him all at once and pumping the wounds full of deadly venom.

He looked at a branch that ran right past his face. It shook, making a rattling sound.

So did other branches.

Shika-shika-shika-sshhhh.

Jermaine twisted, trying to break free. The branches tightened. The whole hill filled with rattling as every bush shook. Thorns dug through his clothes, piercing his flesh. The branches tightened across his chest, keeping him from screaming again. The ground beneath him pulsed as the roots shivered in anticipation.

As the branches pulled him down to the ground, Jermaine learned there are far worse things in the woods than snakes.

∫MART LITTLE ∫UCKER∫

If my dad wasn't so lazy, he would have cut down the tire swing years ago. But the swing stayed where it was, dangling from the old apple tree, long after I'd lost interest in it. Dad hadn't drilled drain holes in the tire, either. Which is why it had a bunch of gross, slimy water in the bottom. Stagnant water—that's what you call it. I didn't know that when I first encountered the little suckers. I learned it later. Anyhow, insects love stagnant water—especially mosquitoes.

The first time I got bitten, I was in the backyard with my friend Arnold, flying balsa-wood airplanes. I glanced down at my arm just in time to see the insect flit away. It looked like a mosquito, except it was green.

"Shoot," I said, scratching at my arm.

"What's wrong?" Arnold asked.

"I got bit."

"Bitten," he said. Arnold was always correcting me. It was a pain, but it was his only bad habit, so I put up with it.

I noticed some more bugs near the tire swing. "Come on,

let's go out front." I didn't want to get bit—I mean bitten—again.

But the next day, I had to go in the backyard to get my soccer ball. I got another bite. Same kind of green bug. This time I managed to smack it before it took off. One less bug to bite people.

I took my soccer ball over to Arnold's house. But he didn't want to kick it around, because he was all wrapped up in making this computer game.

"Can I try it?" I asked.

"I guess. But it's not all working yet. And it's way too easy."

"I don't care." I sat down at the keyboard and clicked the mouse cursor on the START button. A rocket ship came out of the left side of the screen. Enemies came out of the right side.

A couple of the enemy ships froze in the middle of the screen. "I'm still working on the motion routines," Arnold said. "The delta X value for acceleration keeps getting cleared, and I don't know why."

I didn't bother responding to that, since I had no idea what he meant. Instead, I started shooting the enemies. In a couple seconds, I wiped out the first wave. "You're right. It's pretty easy."

"After I get it working, I'll make it harder."

I was racking up an awesome score. And I kept winning extra ships. Before I knew it, I had fifty ships. And then eighty. A little later, I was all the way up to ninety-nine.

"Cool," I said. "Watch me get one hundred ships."

"Uh-oh . . . ," Arnold said as I blasted away at more enemies.

"What's wrong?" As I asked that, I won my one hundredth ship. But instead of *100*, the display showed *0*. And the GAME OVER message popped up. "Why'd that happen?"

"It wrapped around back to zero," he said.

I didn't get it. Math wasn't my best thing. "What do you mean?"

"I only used two digits for the number of ships. So after ninety-nine, when it reached one hundred, all the program saw was zero-zero. It thought you were out of ships."

"I still don't get it," I said.

"Never mind."

I let it go. I hung out for a while longer and listened as Arnold tried to explain other computer-programming stuff to me, like how he had to tell the difference between when you held a key down and when you hit it a bunch of times. None of that made much sense to me, either.

When I got home, I made the mistake of putting my soccer ball in the backyard. That earned me another bite. The next day, we had a test on complex fractions, which I really don't understand. Except, I sort of understood everything this time. The questions didn't seem all that hard.

Over the next two or three weeks, I found myself understanding more and more of the stuff my teachers talked about—not just math, but science and English, too. I was grasping things that made no sense to me before. I even finally understood what Arnold had been trying to tell me about the keyboard, and about the ninety-nine ships. It was like when my dad rolled the miles on his old car. It went from 99,999 to 0.

I was definitely getting smarter. Day by day. At a fast rate. By the end of the month, I was smart enough to figure out what was happening. It was the bugs. Something in their bite was raising my intelligence. There are lots of examples of this sort of cooperation in nature. It's called *symbiosis*. Two organisms help each other. Each gains something. I provided the insects with nutrients—specifically, my blood—and they, in turn, provided me with greater intelligence.

I made sure to go out to the backyard each day. Then Dad started talking about getting rid of the tire swing. I couldn't let that happen.

"I'll take care of it," I said. I was smart enough to know he'd leap at the offer.

"You sure you can handle it?" he asked.

"No problem. I'll get Arnold to help me." But I was planning to do it by myself. I didn't want Arnold getting bitten and catching up with me. I was already a lot smarter than he was. I knew how to fix all sorts of mistakes in his computer program. Not that I told him. I didn't want to show off, or have him wonder how I got so smart.

I took our stepladder out back. Then I propped some cinder blocks under the tire so it wouldn't fall when I sliced the rope. After I cut the tire down, I carried it out to the edge of the backyard and stuck it behind a hedge where nobody would notice it. The stagnant water sloshed, and a bit of it spilled, but there was plenty left to provide a nice breeding ground for my symbiotic pals.

Perfect. The bugs were safe, and I could continue to grow smarter. I must have gotten bitten at least fifty times while I was moving the tire. But that was fine. I could feel my intelligence swelling and growing.

I headed toward the house. But I then realized there was no reason to grow smarter a little at a time. I wanted to do it in one huge dose. So I went back, took off my shirt, and sat by the tire.

They swarmed over me. I grew even smarter. Pretty soon, I knew I was the smartest kid in the world. And then the smartest person.

How high can I go? I wondered. Was there a limit? Would I reach a maximum, and then stay there? I contemplated the enigma of an upper limit to intelligence. Even finite things can appear infinite if the upper boundary is sufficiently distant.

And then my ultrasuperbrilliant mind had another thought. What if my brain had only a certain capacity for intelligence? Or what if my IQ reached 999? Was it possible that my intelligence could wrap back to zero, like the number of extra lives in Arnold's game?

That was too much of a risk. I was smart enough. I got up, batted the bugs away from me, and walked toward the house. I felt dazzlingly brilliant. I understood problems in math and science that nobody had ever been able to figure out. I saw a five-step proof of Fermat's theorem and a beautifully elegant way to confirm the four-color map theorem.

And then I felt a click, like a counter was turning over in my brain.

Huh? What? Why am I here? I itch. "Momeee!" I screamed. There were bugs out here. Bad bugs. *I'll ask Daddy to kill them.* I ran inside, where I would be safe from all those stupid bugs.

OVERDUE ONTO OTHER*S*

Edith had gone to the library to look for the latest book in a mystery series she was hooked on. They didn't have it, so she browsed around a bit. She finally found a couple other books that looked interesting, including a graphic novel. As she was heading toward the circulation desk, she noticed a shelf under the videos with a sign that read: PERSONALITIES. CHECK ONE OUT TODAY!

That's weird, Edith thought. *Maybe it's something about celebrities.* The shelf held a row of small plastic cases, about half the size of the ones movies come in. Each case had a label on the side. Most were just a word or two. ADVENTUROUS, OUTGOING, FUN-LOVING, POPULAR. Stuff like that. It wasn't all good stuff. There were a whole bunch with labels like LOSER, COWARD, CRYBABY, and other things Edith wouldn't want to be.

She grabbed the one labeled POPULAR and took it up to the desk.

"What's this?" she asked the librarian.

"Personalities," she said. "It's the latest thing. We're the first library in the county to offer them."

"Oh. Right." Edith didn't want to admit that she still had no idea what it was, so she checked it out with her books.

As soon as she left the library, she opened the case. There was nothing inside except for a stretchy wristband—the kind people wear to show they're against a disease or in favor of some sort of cause. Except, instead of rubber, this was made out of braided wire.

Edith slipped the band onto her wrist, then stood there for a moment, trying to sense any change. *This is silly.* She knew a wristband couldn't make her popular. She sure didn't feel any different.

On the way home, as she passed the playground, a couple girls from her class ran over from the basketball court. "Edith, wait up," they called.

"Come play, Edith."

"She's on our team."

"No, she's on our team."

They fought over her until she shouted, "Stop that!"

"Sure thing, Edith," they all said.

She put her books down and played ball until it was time for dinner.

The next day, Edith got invited to sit at the cool table in the cafeteria. And everyone wanted to be her partner for an art project.

Every day, for three weeks, Edith was popular. Other things changed, too, but not so much. She was a bit bolder than usual, and a bit happier. She realized that each personality band, just like each real personality, contained a mixture of traits, but the strongest was the one listed on the label.

And then the moment she'd dreaded finally came. It was time to take her books back to the library.

She didn't want to return the band. She took it off and left it on her desk. When she handed the books to the librarian, she said, "I lost the personality."

The librarian leaned closer and stared at Edith. "Are you sure it's lost?"

"Absolutely." The funny thing was, Edith knew if she was wearing the band, the librarian would probably believe anything without questioning her. That's how people are treated when they're popular. They can get away with all sorts of stuff. But, without the band, Edith had a hard time even getting people to notice she was alive. That didn't matter. The band was hers now, forever. "Is there a fine?"

"No. That's not our policy." The librarian pointed to a door behind her desk. "Come in the office. We have to fill out a loss report."

That's not so bad. Edith had been afraid she'd have to pay for the personality. She'd fill out reports all day if it meant she didn't have to give up being popular.

Edith followed the librarian into the office. The librarian closed the door and handed Edith a pen. It was attached to a wire, like the pens her parents used to sign for stuff with their credit card. The other end of the wire went inside a black box that was attached to the USB port on a computer.

Edith picked up the pen and looked at the form. The first line asked for the missing title. She wrote, *Popularity*. The rest of the form asked for her name, address, and phone number. At the bottom, there was a box for her to check. *Patron gives the library permission to obtain a replacement?*

Why not? She didn't care what they did. She put a check-mark in the box. The pen got hot all of a sudden. Edith tried to let go, but her fingers curled around it. Her arm started to shake.

It lasted just an instant. Then her fingers fell open and she dropped the pen. The librarian lifted the lid of the black box and pulled out a wristband. She put it in a plastic case. Then she took a label from her printer. Edith noticed one word on it: DISHONEST.

The librarian stuck the label on the case. "That's all. You can go."

Edith got up and stumbled out of the library. The world felt flat and strange, like she wasn't really a part of it. Something important had been sucked out of her.

As she wandered past the playground, she heard kids talking.

"Who's that?"

"Nobody."

"You can say that again. She's a total nothing. She's got no personality at all."

Edith got home just as her mom was taking a garbage bag out to the curb. "I cleaned up some junk on your desk," her mom said. "If I waited for you to do it, it would never happen."

"Whatever." Edith went upstairs and sat on her bed. She had no desire to do anything else. There was really no place she wanted to go. There was really nothing at all she wanted to do. Ever.

PUT ON YOUR HAPPY FACE

I'd made it! I'd been accepted by the world's greatest school for clowns. I'd bet they've never taken a kid before. But I'm good—very good. I can juggle five balls while balancing on a teeterboard. I can even juggle three balls with my eyes closed. I can ride a unicycle, walk on my hands, and take a fall that looks hilarious.

It doesn't matter that I'm only twelve. They accepted me. My aunt and uncle, who I'd been living with, were happy to let me go. They pretended to care about me, but I knew the truth.

None of that mattered.

I was right where I needed to be. Poirotte Clown College— the best clown school in the world. The teachers were so serious about being clowns—yeah, I know it sounds funny saying it that way—anyhow, they're so serious that they always wore their makeup in class.

And each face was different. Most people don't know this, but that's one of the most important decisions a clown has to make. Every clown has his own face. I'd read that in the old days a clown would paint a copy of his makeup on an egg and they'd keep all the eggs in the town hall. I guess it was a way to make sure nobody could steal your face. That was a long time ago, somewhere like France or England.

I loved the college. And I was really good. Some of the students couldn't handle the harder stuff. One poor guy never did get the hang of walking in big shoes. But I nailed every skill on my first try. I was a natural-born clown.

When Emmett—he was my teacher for slapstick class—showed me how to throw a pie, I did it perfectly the first time. Same with the seltzer bottle.

In a week, I was even driving the clown car—and I'm not nearly old enough to drive a real car. It's amazing how many clowns we could pack in it. You've seen that at the circus, I'm sure. Well, it's no trick—just hard work, a lot of planning, and a bit of pain. But I don't even mind some pain. If I take a bad fall or a hard slap, that doesn't matter. I just shake it off and keep going. As long as I can be a clown, I'm happy.

"You've got it, kid," Emmett said to me during my second month. "You were born for this."

"I know," I said. I loved his face. Instead of the usual red nose, he had a long orange one, sort of like Pinocchio. But he had a big smile and stars around his eyes. Emmett was a happy clown.

Smiles are a major decision. Some clowns are happy and some are sad. I want a smile, because I like action and laughter. Sad Sack—he's another of the teachers—has this really sad face, with tears and all. That's great if you're into that, but I like happy faces. Though even the happy faces sort of seem sad sometimes.

Finally, I got to start my makeup class. Instead of putting

the greasepaint on our own faces, they had us work on a dummy. I guess that gave us a better chance to look at it as we experimented.

It took two weeks of playing around, but I finally created the perfect face.

"Is that the one, kid?" Emmett asked.

"Yeah. That's me." It was exactly what I wanted—huge red nose, big smile, blue lines making giant eyebrows. And freckles. Lots of orange freckles. I'd topped it all off with an enormous wig of frizzy green hair. It was great.

"You sure?"

"Absolutely." I could just see the little kids in the audience cracking up when I clomped out with this makeup and a pair of giant shoes, carrying a pie or walking an invisible dog.

"Great," Emmett said. "You did a fine job. Let's take a break." We went to the cafeteria, where he treated me to a special lunch.

I fell asleep right after we ate. I usually don't take a nap, but I just couldn't keep my eyes open that afternoon.

When I woke up, Emmett was there, sitting right by the side of my bed. He held out a mirror.

"Wow," I said. I guess Emmett had put on my makeup. "Perfect." As soon as the words left my lips, a wave of pain washed over my face.

"Easy, kid," Emmett said. "It'll hurt for a few days. But then you'll be fine."

"Hurt?" I asked. Even that small word caused my lips to ache. I reached up to touch my big red nose.

Emmett grabbed my wrist. "Leave it alone. Let it heal."

Heal? I stared in the mirror at the clown face I'd created.

A face that would last forever. It wasn't makeup. It was my own flesh—carved and reformed to match my design. That's when I knew why even the funniest clown, with the biggest smile, sometimes seems to have a sad, sad face behind the makeup.

MOODS

Look what I found," Colleen said as she slipped into her seat at school. She held out her hand, revealing the treasure that lay on her palm.

"Nice ring," Madeleine said.

"It's not just a ring," Colleen told her. "It's special. My grandma got it ages ago, when she was a kid. Watch this." Colleen slipped the ring on her finger and waited while the large stone reacted.

"Wow," Madeleine said. "It changed colors."

"Yeah. Grandma said they call it a mood ring. It's so cool."

"Can I try?" Madeleine asked.

"Sure." Colleen handed the ring over, then watched as the color of the stone shifted from blue to green on Madeleine's finger.

"What's the color mean?" Madeleine asked.

Colleen shrugged. "Grandma couldn't remember."

"Hey, what's up?" Lindsey asked, leaning over Madeleine's shoulder.

Colleen explained, and Lindsey tried the ring. Then

Cathy tried, along with all the rest of the girls in the class. Except for Deanne. She just sat in the back like she always did, not really taking part. Ever since she'd shown up, a month and a half ago, the girls had tried to get to know her, but she hadn't responded to their attempts. She seemed more like a spectator than a student.

"I know," Colleen said, "let's find out Deanne's mood." She went to Deanne's desk at the far right side of the last row and held out the ring.

Deanne just sat there, not looking up.

"Come on," Colleen said. "Try it. It's fun." She could feel the other girls gathering behind her.

Deanne still didn't move.

"Oh, come on. Be a sport." Colleen reached out and lifted Deanne's hand, then slipped the ring on the girl's finger.

The stone lost all color.

Colleen pulled the ring free.

"What happened?" Madeleine asked from behind Colleen. "I didn't see."

"Yeah," Lindsey said, "I didn't see, either."

"It turned red," Colleen said. She wasn't exactly sure why she'd lied, but she had a feeling she'd stumbled across a sad and painful secret.

Deanne moved her lips slightly, as if silently whispering, *Thank you.*

"We'd better get to our seats before class starts." Colleen walked away from Deanne, not looking back.

Deanne didn't come to school the next day. Or ever again. Colleen never forgot the clear lifeless look of the gem in the mood ring, or the cold lifeless feel of Deanne's fingers. And she never wore the ring again.

KEEP YOUR *SPIRITS* UP

I only did one truly stupid thing in my entire life. That was enough. It killed me. One minute, I'm proving I'm brave enough to slip out of my harness and stand up while riding the tallest, fastest roller coaster in the state. The next minute, I'm floating over my body. Truly stupid. Terminally stupid.

It wasn't much fun watching the rest. My buddy Rick scrambled out of the coaster the normal way, at the end of the ride. He ran over and pushed through the crowd that had gathered a safe distance from the spray zone of my splattered remains. When he saw my body, he turned away and got sick. I can't blame him.

I felt kind of numb. I mean, there I was, being scraped into an ambulance—as if there was any point taking me to a hospital—but here I was drifting around like a jellyfish at high tide.

"Hey, what's your name?"

I turned and saw someone drifting toward me. He looked about my age. I could see through him. I held up my hand and stared at it. I could see through that, too.

"Your name?" he asked again.

"Brett," I said. "Am I a ghost?"

"Yup. You're a ghost. Congratulations on figuring that out. Some people have a hard time with the concept. After the way you flew out of that ride, I figured you might not be the brightest guy around. I'm Curtis."

"Hi," I said. "Now what?"

"We hang out, or we drift around. Come on—I'll introduce you to some of the guys and girls who hang out here." Curtis started to drift away.

"Hey," I called after him. "How do I move?"

"Just kind of lean forward," he said. "Like with one of those electric scooters."

I tilted myself. It worked. I drifted with Curtis to the other side of the park. He introduced me to five kids—I mean, ghosts—who were in the amusement park at the time. They were pretty nice, though they all mentioned that my last act as a living person had been pretty much the stupidest thing they'd seen in a long time. I didn't argue with them. After that, I just drifted around the park for a while.

That night, Curtis came looking for me. There were three other ghosts with him. "Hey, Brett, I have to ask you something. That kid Rick—the one who was on the coaster with you—he's a friend of yours. Right?"

"Yeah. He's my best friend. I mean, he was. . . ."

"Well, Rick's going to have a bad accident tonight. He's going to die unless you stop him from leaving his house."

"How do you know that?"

"We can see this stuff," Terry, another of the ghosts, told me. "You will, too, once you've been here for a while. Your buddy is going to walk out of his house and head down the street. When he reaches the corner, a power line's going to break and the wire is going to fall right on him. Zap! Bye, bye, Rick."

"What can I do?" I asked. "Can I stop him?"

"Sure," Curtis said. "We can appear to people if we try really hard. It just takes a lot of energy."

I didn't wait to hear any more. I drifted as fast as I could toward Rick's house. I hoped I wasn't too late. I didn't want him to get fried, even though it would be nice to have him around here all the time.

As I got closer, I realized I hadn't asked when Rick's accident was supposed to happen. I waited a long time. At least I didn't get hungry or thirsty. Just bored. Finally, the front door opened, and Rick came down his porch steps. He looked awful, like he'd been crying. I felt bad for him, but glad that he missed me.

I drifted in front of him and started shouting. "Go back! Rick, get back. Don't go out."

He walked through me. I drifted ahead of him again and tried harder. "Stop, Rick!"

He hesitated for an instant, as if he'd caught a glimpse of me. Then he shook his head and started walking again. I'd done something right that time. I just hadn't done it hard enough.

"*Stop!*" I shouted, focusing all my strength, wishing with all my concentration that he could see me. The effort took so much out of me that I could feel myself wilt. But it worked.

Rick froze for a moment. His eyes grew wide. Then he screamed and ran back into the house.

I'd saved him. My death, as stupid as it was, had actually served a purpose. For the first time since I died, I felt good.

Behind me, someone laughed.

Curtis was standing in the road, along with about twenty other ghosts—all laughing hysterically.

"Man, oh man, did you see his eyes?" Curtis said.

"I think Rick is putting on clean underwear," Terry said.

"But I saved him. Right?" I asked. "He won't get hit by the power line."

Curtis laughed so hard, he bent over. At the same time, he pointed a finger up above our heads. I looked up. For a moment, I had no idea what I was supposed to see. Then I realized there was something I didn't see. I guess I really can be stupid at times. And not just on roller coasters. There are power lines near my house. Lots of power lines. But Rick lives in a newer section of town. There aren't any power lines overhead in Rick's neighborhood. The lines all run underground.

I shook my head, amazed that Curtis had tricked me so easily. But I guess every group has some sort of tricks or pranks they play on newcomers. My first year at camp, I'd gone on a snipe hunt. I'd stood for an hour in a field, holding a cloth sack, waiting to catch a snipe. It turned out there was no such thing. Instead of heading into the woods to flush the snipe toward me, the other kids had just gone back to camp, looted my locker, and poured maple syrup on my sheets.

"Got you good, didn't we?" Curtis asked.

"Yeah. You got me." There was no point being a bad sport.

"Come on. Let's go back to the park," Curtis said. "Maybe someone will fall off the sky ride."

"Sounds good." As I drifted along next to him, I started thinking up a good trick to play on the next newcomer. It really helped pass the time.

STING, WHERE IS THY DEATH?

Billy didn't even see the attackers until after the searing pain shot through his arm. As he slapped at his shoulder and spun around, he spotted three of them hovering a foot away. Hornets! No mistake. No other stinging creature had that same awful, drooping body, like some sort of half-dead insect that lived only to cause anguish.

He raced for his front door, stumbled over a rock, and fell hard. That's the last thing he remembered before he woke up in the hospital with a cast on his ankle and a bandage on his head.

"Am I okay?" he asked.

"You'll be fine," his mom said, patting his shoulder. "The doctor said it was a clean break."

"How'd it happen?" his dad asked. "When we found you, you were knocked out cold."

Billy explained about the hornets.

"Must be a nest nearby," his dad said. "I'll take care of it this evening. That's the best time to spray a nest, when it's cool outside."

"As long as I can watch them die," Billy said. He pictured the hornets dropping lifelessly to the ground as the spray washed over them.

They brought him home and set him on the couch. A little while later, his dad came inside and said, "I found the nest."

That evening, balancing on crutches, Billy watched as his dad got ready to use the spray.

"Is that stuff good?" Billy asked.

"It's death in a can," his dad said. "It can shoot twenty-five feet straight up. Watch this." He pointed the can at the nest, which was under the roof, right above Billy's bedroom window.

Billy shuddered at the thought that all those hornets had been living so close to him, building their papery home against his own.

His dad pushed the button on top of the can. The liquid inside shot out in a powerful stream. As cool as the spray was, the result wasn't all that exciting. When the first blast hit the nest, a couple hornets escaped. They dropped to the ground, lifeless and wet. Billy wanted to crush them with his good foot, but he wasn't going to walk under the nest. As the poisonous spray coated the nest and expanded into a foam, nothing else escaped.

"All dead," Billy's dad said as the last drops dribbled from the canister.

"Good." Billy imagined the hornets, trapped in the dark, dying a sudden and unexpected death. He couldn't help smiling. Maybe later, they could knock the nest down and burn it. The dead insects would crackle like popcorn. The thought made Billy happy. He put his weight on his good foot, leaned over, and grabbed a rock. He hurled it at the nest, knocking a small hole in the bottom. Nothing flew out.

"Nice shot, sport," his dad said.

"Now get to bed," his mom said. "You need to rest up so you can heal."

The next day, Billy's ankle hurt too much for him to walk, so he stayed in bed. That evening, his creepy cousin Amy came to visit him.

"What are you doing here?" he asked.

"I'm going to mend you," she said. She held up a paper bag. "I've been doing research in natural healing."

Billy didn't say anything. He'd learned there was no point talking to Amy when she became obsessed with a new hobby. It was easier to let her do what she wanted. She was annoying, but harmless. Last year, she'd decided to save endangered species. Then, she'd gotten all crazy about an online multi-player game and made everyone call her Etherea the Enchantress. After that wore off, she started looking for flying saucers. Now, apparently, she was some sort of mystical healer.

She pulled a candle, a metal bowl, and a bunch of small jars from a bag and put everything on Billy's bedside table. "These are healing elements," she said, pointing to the jars. "Essence of hyacinth picked under the new moon, myrtle from a sacred grove, rust from a piece of iron two centuries old."

She kept talking, but Billy tuned her out. After she opened all the jars, she placed the bowl on a small stand above the candle.

Amy lit the candle. "Let the healing begin."

"Does your mom know you're playing with matches?" Billy asked.

"I'm not playing," Amy said. "This is serious. Women have practiced healing arts since the beginning of time." She emptied the contents of each of the jars into the bowl.

Smoke trickled from the mixture. Just little wisps drifted out at first. Then, with a *whumpf,* the mixture ignited. Thick plumes rose from the bowl.

"Put it out!" Billy shouted.

"Relax," Amy said. "It's almost finished. You need to stay still so the healing vapors can penetrate your cast."

There was a bright orange flash from the bowl, followed by a final dense cloud of smoke. Billy couldn't breathe. He could hardly see. Coughing, he tumbled out of bed, winced as his bad foot touched the floor, then raised the cast off the ground, hopped to the wall, and opened his window.

Fresh air flowed in and the awful smoke seeped out. Billy gasped, steadying himself with one hand against the wall.

"It won't work if you do that," Amy said.

"It won't work anyhow!" Billy shouted. "It's ridiculous. And you're crazy. Just get out. Go save some endangered dolphins or something."

"Well, if that's how you feel about my help, I'm leaving." Amy blew out the candle, gathered everything, and left the room.

"Idiot," Billy muttered. As he turned back toward the bed, something buzzed past his face.

Hornet! he realized. One of them must have been away when the nest was sprayed. He slammed the window closed, just in case there were more stragglers. Then he grabbed his math book from his desk and looked around for the hornet. There it was, on the wall right next to the door. "You're dead." He hopped across the room and slammed the book against the insect, flattening it.

He pulled the book away and looked with satisfaction at the crushed remains, still stuck to the book.

"I win." Billy dropped the book to the floor, then went back to bed. His ankle hurt like crazy. As he stretched out, a motion caught his eye. He looked at the book on the floor.

Billy blinked. He was sure the smoke had messed up his eyes. He blinked again. But there was no mistake. The crushed hornet started to wriggle and twitch.

It lifted its head from the book. Its thorax expanded. As the stinger regained its shape, Billy leaped from the bed, grabbed the book, and slammed it against the wall. Again and again, he hit it. Finally, out of breath, barely able to see anything past the sweat stinging his eyes, he looked at the book. The hornet was beyond crushed. All that was left was a smeared streak of insect paste.

As the adrenaline faded from his bloodstream, Billy's leg crumpled. The pain, worse than anything before, knocked him off his feet. He fell, dropping the book. As he lay there, he saw the jellied smear of hornet quiver again. It started to pull together.

I'll throw the book outside, he thought. That would be enough for now. Whatever Amy's healing smoke had done, he'd toss the hornet outside and be safe. As much as his leg throbbed, he knew he could make it across the room. Billy looked at the window and frowned.

It was dark.

Too dark.

No streetlights shone through. No moonlight. The darkness flowed and pulsed like a living creature. Billy heard taps against the glass. Light taps, at first. Then harder ones. Hundreds of taps.

The hornets, Billy realized. Healed. Back from the dead. Unkillable. Pressing against the glass. Ramming it like hailstones. Amy's healing smoke had seeped into the hive.

A crack shot across one of the windowpanes.

Billy pushed himself to his feet, trying to ignore the bursts of agony that exploded through his ankle. He turned toward his door.

Behind him, he heard the sharp crack of glass breaking. The hornets swarmed inside. Billy raced for the door, but he never reached it.

A WORD OR TWO ABOUT THESE STORIES

As always, here's a look at where I got my ideas. I should warn those of you who like to read this part first that there are some spoilers in the explanations.

All the Rage
One of my main sources for ideas is my "what if" file. Each day, I jot down a what-if question. The file is currently sixty-two pages long, single spaced, with more than 1,100 ideas in it, not counting the ideas I've used and removed. This story was inspired by the simple question, "What if there was a kid who never got angry?" I enjoy writing stories about the one kid in a class who is different in some way. (See "The Boy Who Wouldn't Talk" from *In the Land of the Lawn Weenies* for another example of this.)

Frankendance
Every dad wants to find the perfect guy for his daughter. I couldn't help thinking how much easier that would be if

you could make the guy. I liked the idea of a dad doing that. And I'm a fan of the original *Frankenstein* movie. As for the rest of the story, I'm as surprised as anyone by what happened once they got to the dance.

The Ratty Old Bumbershoot
I think I was fighting an umbrella in a windstorm when this idea hit me. Umbrellas do seem to be alive when they start flapping and twisting. They sort of remind me of bats, though that's not quite the direction this story took. As for *bumbershoot,* it's such a wonderfully silly word that I had to use it.

Dear Author
I love getting real fan letters, but I also sometimes get letters that are obviously a classroom assignment. They almost always have the same form—three things I like about your book, three questions, and so on. I don't know how all of this started, but I think it would be so much better if students were assigned to write to someone in their community or to someone who doesn't get much mail.

The Wizard's Mandolin
I was tuning my guitar and thinking about sharp and flat notes when the idea for this story hit me. I also own a mandolin, but I don't play it very well. (I own a banjo, too, but I'm pretty sure "The Wizard's Banjo" wouldn't have had the sort of feel I was looking for.) I had fun with the viewpoint of this one. It's nice writing things in different styles.

Into the Wild Blue Yonder

I hate to admit that I got the idea for the ending first. I just envisioned a carnival ride turning into something much less pleasant. I'm not sure what that says about my mind. Then, I had the fun task of creating someone worthy of being put on that ride.

Yackity-Yak

Another gift from my what-if pile. Originally, I was going to use a magic ring. But a book of spells made more sense. It's fun to write a story once in a while that has just one person speaking, without any descriptions or any dialogue from other characters. Given the plot of this story, I couldn't think of a better time to let one character do all the talking. This is another reason I love short stories. You can experiment and do all sorts of things that might not work in a novel.

Wish Away

I'm not the first (or the seven hundredth) person to write a story about wishes being granted. I've had at least two wish stories in earlier collections ("Anything You Want" and "The Genie of the Necklace"). This particular story started out with the idea, "What if anyone could wish things away from anyone else?" I tweaked the idea a bit, to limit who was doing the taking. That happens a lot. An idea won't be quite right for some reason, but I'll play with it and work around the parts that are causing a problem.

The Department Store

I had no idea where this one was going when I started. I wanted to have a kid stay in a store overnight. And I wanted it to be creepy. Given how creepy mannequins are, I'm not surprised what happened. Though I hope you were.

The Battle of the Red Hot Pepper Weenies
I started with the idea of a pair of kids getting into a pepper-eating contest. There's just something about hot peppers that makes people abandon common sense. I guess the same could be said for lots of other things that inspire people to compete. I like hot peppers, but I always try to stop eating them somewhere between tears and flames.

Just Like Me
I remember seeing a magazine ad for a place where they make dolls that looks just like people. That struck me as potentially creepy. I definitely wouldn't want to be anywhere near a doll that looked like me. Naturally, anything creepy is worth thinking about for story inspirations. I combined that idea with one about people who treat their dolls a little too much like they are real.

What's Eating the Vegans?
I know lots of vegetarians. I like them, but I also like making fun of them, because I'm really not a nice person, and I'm envious of their excellent health. I also thought it would be fun to put vegetarians in the middle of a Thanksgiving dinner. I'd originally envisioned an attack of giant vegetables, but common sense prevailed and I took a different direction.

Let's Have a Big Hand for Gerald
Once in a while, I like to write a story that is flat-out absurd. (See "Throwaways" in *Invasion of the Road Weenies*.)

My spark here was, "What if a kid's hand kept growing bigger?" Actually, the fact that Gerald's hand keeps growing isn't the absurd part. For me, his mom's reaction is what makes the story deliciously bizarre. The nice thing about what-ifs is that an idea could turn into so many different types of stories. On another day, Gerald might have found himself elbow deep in dark horror, or performing some sort of heroic high five. This time around, I sent him somewhere else.

Bird Shot

I came up with the ending first. That's obviously the ideal way to make sure the story will have an ending. It's easier to work backwards by asking, "How did things get this way?" than to work forward by asking, "What happened next?" On the other hand, if I don't know the ending when I start writing, there's a better chance it will be a nice surprise for me and for the reader. Either way, it's my job to make sure the path to the ending is as satisfying as the ending itself. This means I have to make the ending feel both believable and satisfying. (If a counselor showed up and took away the BB gun, that would be believable, but not very satisfying. If the ground opened up and swallowed the kid, that would be satisfying, but not believable.)

The Princess and the Pea Brain

I'm pleased to admit that the whole idea was inspired by the title. Wordplay is constantly dancing through my head. When I thought up the title, it wasn't hard to imagine what kind of fate would happen to a pea-brained prince if he found himself in this sort of story.

Petro-fied

It's hard not to think about gas and oil these days. This is another case where I knew from the start how the story would end. I just didn't know the rest of it right away. True confession—I was doing the final edit of the story, and these notes, right after five inches of snow fell. I just filled the tank of my snowblower. Right now, my fingers smell like gasoline. I would never buy a snowblower, but my favorite lawn weenie gave me his when he moved to Florida.

Time Out

This one was totally unplanned. I just tossed a couple kids in a room with a time machine to see what would happen. Time travel can get pretty tricky for writers (and readers). The classic example of a time-travel paradox is this: What if you went back in time and prevented your grandfather from meeting your grandmother? Would you cease to exist? Nobody really has a good answer for this. My story went in a different direction, but it is still probably one of the harder ones to wrap your mind around.

Galactic Zap

This was sort of a combined what-if and ending idea. The what-if part gave me the idea for a game that was actually a screening test. At the same time, the reason for the screening gave me the ending. I wasn't sure whether to include this story, since the story "Inquire Within" from my previous collection also dealt with a screening test, though in an entirely different way. That's actually the greatest challenge of putting together a collection—making sure that any particular sort of twist doesn't happen too often. I decided to keep this one in because I love the last line. If you want to read the best novel ever written about kids fighting aliens, check out *Ender's Game* by Orson Scott Card.

The Taste of Terror
Yup—another what-if. "What if there was a witch who ate screams?" In my first draft, the main character didn't survive. But that didn't feel right. The story was so dark, I felt it needed a happy ending.

The Cat Almost Gets a Bath
I read a magazine article about bathing cats to reduce allergies. Having actually bathed a cat once or twice for various reasons (don't try this at home), I knew how dangerous and frantic an exercise it could become. It struck me as an ideal topic for a funny story.

Yesterday Tomorrow
This is really another version of a time-travel story, though quite different from "Time Out." I'm working on a third time-travel story, with an entirely different sort of ending, but I figured I'd save that for the next collection. This one began with, "What if a kid woke up a day earlier each day?" That, as interesting as it might be, didn't strike me as enough, by itself, for a story. But, as I thought about what his life would be like, and realized the things he could do, I saw the chance for a strong ending.

Take a Whack at This
Another story that began as a what-if. I'm actually quite fond of spiders. But the ones that show up in my stories tend

not to be all that pleasant. I figure E. B. White has already given us the ultimate nice spider, but there's lots of room to explore the icky side.

King of the Hill

I started with the line that is spoken by the hill. I knew I wanted to put it in a story. At first, I thought the whole thing would just be about some kids playing king of the hill. Then I realized I had to make the story a bit larger.

Book Banning

Writers spend a lot of time dealing with the issue of book banning. So it's not surprising that I was thinking about those two words. Whenever I think about words, I end up playing with them. I wondered what would happen if, instead of being banned, the books did the banning. I have a feeling my librarian friends are going to especially enjoy this one.

Braces

Given how much it cost for my daughter to get braces, there was no way I wasn't going to write a story about it sooner or later. In this case, it was later. She's had her braces off for years. But I still remember sitting with her in the waiting room. And I still remember way back in the dark ages when I got braces myself. But that's another story.

Turkey Calls

I wondered what would happen if a kid made a turkey call and it called something else. Of course, that's just the start of the process. I needed to make it seem reasonable that the call wouldn't work right, and maybe give a hint that what-ever came might not be a bird.

Reel
This began with, "What if a kid felt everything that hap-pened in a movie?" The first time I started to write that story, I got sidetracked and ended up writing about a kid who sees himself in a play ("Alexander Watches a Play"). This time, I stuck with the idea.

Bad Luck
I liked the idea of personifying an aspect of fate. (That sen-tence was an attempt to raise the reading level of this book. This would be a good time to put the book down and say to whoever told you not to buy such a silly book, "Hey—I'm learning about personification as a rhetorical device. This book is very educational, even if there are Weenies on the cover.") There have been lots of stories where Death is a character. I wanted to spend some time with something less drastic. Bad Luck seemed like the perfect choice.

Rattled Nerves
I'd been talking with someone about what kinds of danger-ous snakes live in Pennsylvania. That conversation settled into my brain and led me to think about a kid who believes he's being chased by a venomous snake. Then, I had to think up something that would be mistaken for a snake, but would be much worse. (I guess I could have gone in the op-posite direction and had it turn out he was running from something that wasn't dangerous.) That's where the fun stuff happens. Writing this type of story is sort of like doing

a magic trick. I have to keep you from noticing the surprise until the end.

Smart Little Suckers

The idea for the insects came first. I knew they would make someone smarter. I didn't know what would happen after that. As for the rolling-over part, I actually did make that mistake in one of my early video games, *The Challenge of Nexar* for the Atari 2600. After I programmed it and the cartridge got shipped to stores, someone complained that when he won one hundred ships, the game ended. I never expected anyone to do that well, so I hadn't bothered to make sure the number didn't wrap back to zero. I fixed it, and we made more cartridges. This just shows that any mistakes you make can come in handy later on.

Overdue onto Others

Every time I go to my local library in Nazareth, they seem to have new things you can borrow. This is great, but it got me thinking about what sort of things they could offer in the future. At the same time, I was playing around with an idea that was inspired by a sign I saw at a computer show. The sign read: WE BUY AND SELL MEMORIES. I only wrote a paragraph or two for that one, but it helped lead me toward the concept of doing something with personalities.

Put on Your Happy Face

This is sort of a companion piece to my story "Mr. HooHaa!" from *The Curse of the Campfire Weenies*. It looks at the general creepiness of clowns from the opposite direction. I'm not afraid of clowns, but I definitely like spiders better.

Moods

I was thinking about mood rings one day. Why was I thinking about mood rings? I have no clue. But I'm glad I was. That thought led me to wonder what would happen if a mood ring didn't show any color. It didn't take me long to think up an answer to that question. The toughest decision with this sort of story is whether to go into all sorts of detail and stretch things out, or just get right to the ending. I like how this one feels at this length. As Lincoln said, a story only needs to be long enough to reach the ending.

Keep Your Spirits Up

I was thinking about how every group has some sort of initiation or ritual for new members. I just took that concept and applied it to the ultimate (or perhaps, final) group someone might join. The actual cause of death could have been anything, but since I'm a roller coaster fan, I figured I'd pick something spectacular. (If you're reading this book on the way to an amusement park, you have my apology.)

Sting, Where Is Thy Death?

I wanted to create some undead insects. It took a bit of work to put everything in place. That can be one of the harder tasks for a writer. The story can't feel contrived. Everything has to feel natural. That's a lot easier in a novel, where you can take as much space as you need to set things up. But any time I get to write a scene where a mushed piece of insect paste starts to regain its shape, I'm happy.

So, that brings us to the end of another collection. But, happily, not to the end of my short stories. I have more warped and creepy tales in the works, including a vampire story that is so dark, it makes me grin, and encounters with such horrors as scorpions, dolls' heads, Botox, and cat litter. I can't say for sure which stories will make the final cut, but I can promise to do my best to make you laugh, scream, shiver, and gasp the next time we get together.

David Lubar grew up in Morristown, New Jersey. His books include *Hidden Talents*, an ALA Best Book for Young Adults; *True Talents*; *Flip*, a VOYA Best Science Fiction, Fantasy, and Horror selection; and the short-story collections *In the Land of the Lawn Weenies*, *Invasion of the Road Weenies*, and *The Curse of the Campfire Weenies*. He lives in Nazareth, Pennsylvania. You can visit him on the Web at www.davidlubar.com.

READER'*s* GUIDE

ABOUT THIS GUIDE

The information, activities, and discussion questions that follow are intended to enhance your reading of *The Battle of the Red Hot Pepper Weenies*. Please feel free to adapt these materials to suit your needs and interests.

WRITING AND RESEARCH ACTIVITIES

I. Twisting Tales
From inverted quotations to twisted clichés to warped renditions of classic tales, David Lubar goes beyond wordplay to phrase-play, plot-play, and whole-new-worlds-play to create his stories. Try writing some two-to-four page stories using the Lubar-style activities and prompts below. Then, invite friends or classmates to see what kinds of stories they can create using the favorite prompt you choose for them.

▲. Ask a teacher, family member, or friend to give you one piece of good advice, such as "Don't play in the street."

Then write a story in which taking this good advice has some very bad consequences.

B. Like *King of the Hill,* make up a simple game with a ball, a racket, and a safety cone (or other common sports gear)—four rules maximum. Give your game a cool name, teach it to friends or classmates, and play a few rounds. Then invite your friends to discuss what they liked and did not like about the game. Was it too hard to win? Too easy to gang up? Too tempting to cheat? Then write a creepy story about a game in which nobody winds up a winner.

C. Clean your room (or at least pick it up a little). As you clean, set aside several objects that you thought were lost for good, did not know you owned, or caught your attention for another reason. When you finish cleaning, sit holding one of the found objects in your hand and pay close attention to the smells, colors, and sounds around you and to the random thoughts that enter your mind. Then, write a spooky story in which your found object plays a key role.

D. Open a book of poetry, an instructional manual, or other interesting volume to a random page. Scan the page for a curious or amusing phrase or sentence. Then use some version of this phrase as the title for a story—and write it.

E. Go to the children's section of your local library and choose a picture book. After reading the story, write your own spine-tingling version. Or rewrite the ending of your favorite novel with a creepy twist.

II. Putting Words into Action

Many stories in this collection explore what happens when a character takes action to fulfill a secret wish or desire. Is it okay to feel jealous or angry as long as you do not act on the emotion? Should you talk about these feelings before they get out of hand?

A. Talking too much, or perhaps not enough, plays an important role in several tales. Hold a talk-a-thon in your classroom or community. Invite teams of people to converse without stopping for a period of time. Make sure to agree upon rules for breaks, if any, and how a winner or winners will be declared. If desired, provide a list of conversation topics on index cards, and water of course! Afterward, discuss how hard or easy it was to talk, talk, talk.

B. To what lengths would you go to be popular? Find at least three stories in the collection in which the desire for popularity is a dangerous motivator. Create a survey about the importance of popularity, the difference between popularity and friendship, and other related topics of your choosing to be completed by classmates or friends. Compile the results on a chart or table and write a short report noting the most surprising results you discover.

C. Several story characters begin their journeys as a result of being angry about or punished for a misdeed. Go to the library or online to learn about positive ways to handle feelings of anger. Discuss strategies for anger management with siblings, friends, teachers, or coaches. Compile the results in a computer-designed booklet entitled "Getting Angry in a Good Way" or a title of your choice. Include a bibliography of your research sources and fun quotations from friends, coaches, and even famous figures quoted about anger.

D. In small groups, select one-to-three stories that seem the most creepy, interesting, or relevant to your community. Bring these stories to life as dramatic readings or grab a video camera and make them into short movies. Present your results to friends or classmates.

E. From "Swallow your rage" to "put on your happy face," clichés gone wild are a key feature of this collection. Go to the library or online to find a definition of the term "cliché." What is valuable about clichés? Why are such phrases worth exploring? What famous historical figures provided the world with unforgettable clichés? On a wall of your school, community center, or home, post a giant sheet of paper (or create a blog or website) entitled "Cliché Central." Invite visitors or passers-by to post their favorite clichés. What can you learn about your friends or community by the clichés they choose?

III. Weenie World

David Lubar has a special talent for exploring ideas central to kids' lives while, at the same time, creating incredible models for short-story writing and for thinking about literature in big, exciting ways. What has this collection made you wonder?

A. Make a list of at least eight key themes explored by stories in this collection, including being angry, talking/not talking, and popularity. In discussion with friends or classmates, or through a vote or survey, order the themes from most important to least important to your life and community. Print up the ranking on a large sheet of paper.

B. From Orson Scott Card's modern classic *Ender's Game* to an inverted biblical expression ("O death, where is thy sting?" (1 Cor. 15:55)) to the long-popular fairy tales "The Princess and the Pea" and "Hansel and Gretel," the author gives familiar scenarios totally twisted outcomes. Read one of the books, passages, or stories above, or another book or story you see reinterpreted in one of Lubar's shorts. Then, write a short essay comparing the two literary works.

C. Find three stories in the novel that explore the notion of following· instructions. Make a list of their titles, main characters, instructions, and the story outcomes. Using your list as inspiration, write your own "Guide to Following Instructions and Avoiding Disaster." Your guide can be useful, comic, or even scary. If desired, turn your completed guide into a PowerPoint presentation or an illustrated brochure to share with friends or classmates.

D. Find a newspaper article about an important environmental, political, or medical concern. Use information from this article to write a scary story in which characters work to fix the problem, or in which characters ignore the issue. Attach the story, the newspaper article, drawings, magazine clippings, or other illustrative elements to a sheet of poster board. Present your poster to classmates or friends before a discussion of the real-life concern.

E. If you have read more than one *Weenie* story collection or other book by David Lubar, make a top-ten list of Lubar's favorite creepy topics. (Hint: Consider clowns and psychic abilities.) Compare two stories from different books that deal with the same subject from the list. What elements do they share? How do the endings differ? What conclusions might you draw about the subject based on your comparison? What might you like to ask the author about this subject?

F. In "Dear Author," a kid finds his story ideas stolen by a mysterious author. Do you think real authors fear getting letters like this? Why or why not? Write a letter to David Lubar.

Tell him which *Red Hot Pepper Weenie* story, or story from another *Weenie* book, you liked the best and why. Which story was the scariest and why? What idea or situation would you suggest Mr. Lubar feature in his next collection?

6. Design a book jacket, poster, T-shirt, or other object celebrating David Lubar's "Weenie World."

QUESTIONS FOR DISCUSSION

1. In "All the Rage," how does the narrator's inability to understand the behavior of a classmate lead him to make a terrifying mistake? Describe the setting and themes of this tale. In what ways do these images and ideas set the stage for the rest of the stories in this collection?

2. "Into the Wild Blue Yonder" and "Yackity-Yak" involve characters that talk too much. Have you ever encountered a very talkative person or found yourself in a situation where you could not stop talking? Describe that situation and how it relates to your reading of these stories.

3. "The Wizard's Mandolin" and "Wish Away" show the risks of using magic to get what you wish. What do you think is the moral of these tales? If you could make one wish (and not for more wishes), for what might you ask? Choose your words carefully and explain why you would make this particular wish.

4. In "The Department Store," does the narrator seem to suffer a fate he does not really deserve? Why or why not? In what other stories do the main characters seem more unlucky than bad? In what stories do you feel the characters got what was coming to them? What are the differences between these two types of tales?

5. Though "The Battle of the Red Hot Pepper Weenies" is unlike most of the other tales in the book because it does not contain a supernatural element, in what ways does it still serve to unify this group of stories?

6. Which stories explore such contemporary notions as veganism and care for animals? What perspectives on these ideas are taken in the stories? Do you agree with these viewpoints? Why or why not?

7. In "King of the Hill" and "Bird Brained," what happens to the characters who begin the stories as bullies? Who are the narrators and how do they react to the events of the stories? What would you have done if you found yourself in the narrators' shoes?

8. In "Just Like Me," "Let's Have a Big Hand for Gerald," and "Braces," parents seem unaware of the mysterious disturbances affecting themselves and their children. Do you ever feel like your parents are just missing the point of a given situation? Compare this feeling to the stories.

9. What kinds of strange powers are found in libraries and books in *Red Hot Pepper Weenies*? Why do you go to the library? Do you enjoy the experience? About what special library object or power might you choose to write a spooky story?

10. "Yesterday Tomorrow" and "Time Out" are two of the stories exploring the consequences of time reversal. Have you ever wished you could turn back the clock? When and why? Has reading these stories changed your mind?

11. "Moods" is one of many stories in which an important young character is dead or dies. What other stories include this feature, and what literary games does the author play with this type of character throughout the collection? Do these stories make you wonder about the possibilities of ghost worlds or other afterlife notions? Explain your answer.

12. "Reel" and "Overdue onto Others" involve objects taking control of characters' lives and experiences. Have you ever believed an object had a special power, such as good luck? Describe this object and your behavior toward it.

13. Is it ever okay to lie? Do liars always get punished? What stories deal with deceit? Do all the characters lie for basically the same reason? What happens to them? What would you do in similar situations?

14. In addition to "Sting, Where Is Thy Death?" what other tales explore the balance between human development and the natural world? Do you worry about this balance in your community? In what ways?

15. Do scary stories help you work through feelings of anger or frustration? Do they make you feel better or worse about the world in which you live? Why is (or isn't) it fun, useful, or even important to have scary stories in your library? What idea, situation, or question do you think more scary stories should be written about today? Explain your answers.